D0458575

7X
8/94

Tuna Fish
Thanksgiving

Tuna Fish Thanksgiving

By C. S. Adler

CLARION BOOKS

New York

Clarion Books
a Houghton Mifflin Company imprint
215 Park Avenue South, New York, NY 10003
Text copyright © 1992 by Carole S. Adler

Library of Congress Cataloging-in-Publication Data

Adler, C.S. (Carole S.)
Tuna fish Thanksgiving / by C.S. Adler.
p.   cm.
Summary: Thirteen-year-old Gilda's parents are getting a
divorce, and she seems to be the only one interested in
keeping the family together and looking out for her younger
brother and sister.
ISBN 0-395-58829-4
[1. Divorce — Fiction.   2. Family problems — Fiction.   3.
Brothers and sisters — Fiction.]   I. Title.
PZ7.A26145Tu   1992   91-615
[Fic] — dc20   CIP   AC

BP   10 9 8 7 6 5 4 3 2 1

To Steven James Adler, who is not only a fine son but a fine man

Sure enough I found Avery fast asleep on the floor between his bed and the starship model he's building. I shook him and said, "Avery, you'll be late for school." Mom had rolled him out of bed before she left for her dress shop, and Dad had called him down to breakfast before he left, but Avery's really hard to wake.

"Miss school again, and the attendance officer'll get you," I threatened.

Avery's eyes popped open. "I'm going."

"When?"

"Don't worry."

"I am worried."

Much as I love my brother, I have to admit he looks like a faded rag doll without his glasses on. The kid's so pale that his blond hair blends right into his long white face. "Come on, Av. Move it."

He grabbed for a chair leg as if I might stand him on his feet and force him into his clothes. I didn't budge, but I was wondering if maybe this school phobia business was a kind of delayed reaction to the parents' divorce announcement. Avery and Bliss had taken it so coolly last summer that I'd figured they just didn't understand our family was about to be chopped up.

Avery, who's eleven, hadn't said a word; he just returned to wherever it is he hangs out in outer space. Bliss, who's eight, had turned to me privately and said, "I don't want to be divorced, Gilda. You tell them."

Well, I had tried. I had argued every evening for a month until Mom forbade me to mention the subject again and said she was sorry she and Dad hadn't just gone ahead and done it on the sly. Not that they could have hidden much from us after the "For Sale" sign was stuck in our front yard.

"Avery, I'm not leaving until you do," I said. He was poking through his drawer for his clothes. To speed him up, I added, "And if I miss taking my earth science test, I could get an F on my report card and have to repeat eighth grade."

"No, you won't. . . . Will you?"

Bright as Avery is, he half believes my tall tales. Now he was looking at me so anxiously that I relented and said, "Not likely. But it could happen, Avery. You never can tell."

Avery takes never-can-tells seriously. "You'd better go," he said. "I'll get dressed. I promise." His eyelid twitched. I knew kids in school teased him because of his tics and twitches. They called him a weirdo. It was a shame for a good kid like him not to have any friends.

"I'll wait downstairs," I told him.

I put on my three-year-old duffle coat. It still fit. I had gotten to be five foot eight at eleven and hadn't grown since, except sideways. But the coat was fraying around the edges. If Mom hadn't been devoting all her time and energy to her dress shop these days, she'd have noticed and bought me a new coat. The House of Flair, that's the name Mom picked when she was seventeen and first started dreaming about owning a dress shop. I wondered if she'd ever dreamed of being a mother. Probably not.

Outside the kitchen door, I stood watching the chilly November wind chase dry leaves across the neighbors' lawns. Ours was the worst lawn on the street, knee high in leaves and grass and full of bare spots. Dad promised to get it in shape before he moved to his girlfriend's house, but he hadn't gotten around to it yet. He hadn't even sorted through his old sports equipment in the garage like Mom asked, which gave me hope that he was in no hurry to leave us.

The middle-school bus driver slowed when she saw me, but I waved her on because Avery can easily get distracted by a book, or an idea for his spaceship model, and forget that he's supposed to be getting dressed. Just yesterday his teacher had sent home a note about his daydreaming and recommended he see a psychologist. Mom pitched the note in the garbage. She said she wasn't going to answer it. "Psychologists can't change a kid's basic nature," she said. "Avery was born a dreamer. He used to forget to suck on the bottle, for cripes sake."

Dad had been doing the dinner dishes, home between tennis clinics at the Indoor Racquet Club where he's the pro. So Mom's remark sparked another battle because of course he had to say, "Well, propping the kid's bottle in a plastic holder made it pretty unappealing, Tina."

Even though Dad's big and broad, he's no match for Mom in a fight. Her family came from near Mount Vesuvius in Italy, and she goes off like a volcano when she gets mad. "So it's my fault Avery's out of it?" she screeched.

"You've never spent much time with him, Tina."

"And what about you? You're supposed to be the great child lover. How much time did you ever spend with him?"

Instead of leaping between them and trying to calm them down the way I usually did, I tried tuning them out that night. That's how Bliss and Avery managed.

Lately, it seemed the parents couldn't have the simplest conversation without fighting. It was as if they really didn't like each other anymore. But shouldn't raising three children have given them enough in common to keep them together? I mean, we're a *family*.

Avery rushed out the kitchen door just in time to catch the elementary school bus on its final run through the neighborhood. His open jacket winged out, and he wasn't wearing gloves or a hat. When his class went outside for recess, he'd freeze. Oh well, he did have his book bag; at least he'd remembered that.

Bliss waved to me from the bus window. She always

got on the school bus on its loop into our development so that she could sit in front. I pointed out that getting on the bus on the first pass made the ride fifteen minutes longer, but Bliss said she didn't care. "I get nauseous if I don't sit on the front seat," she said.

Once Bliss makes up her mind about anything, forget it. For instance, every year since she was four, Bliss has fixed her big brown eyes on Mom and said the only thing she wanted for her birthday was a kitten. This past year Mom — the cat hater — finally broke down and got Bliss a kitten for her eighth birthday. Now Bliss walked around with the kitten draped around her neck or cuddled in the crook of her arm as if it was permanently attached.

I pedaled my bike as fast as I could to keep warm on my way to school. Everyone was in homeroom by the time I arrived. The only noise in the empty halls was my eighth-grade social studies teacher yelling at his group to sit down and pay attention.

The bulletin board facing the front entrance brought me up short. Thanksgiving decorations already? But Dad and I still hadn't cleaned up the garage windows that got soaped Halloween night.

I stared at the clumsy brown construction-paper turkey. Sixth-graders made colorful new tailfeathers for it each year. Every feather gave thanks for something — world peace, a new puppy, a trip to Disneyland, a cure for cancer. One read, "I'm thankful it's my sister who needs the braces."

Suppose Dad moved out before Thanksgiving. How

would our family celebrate? I bit my lip to keep from crying. I love holidays, especially Thanksgiving. Not to be together for it would kill me.

The bell rang for the first class. Instantly the halls turned into a pinball machine with kids whizzing in every direction. Bebe's copper-colored braid flew past me. She backed up and said, "Gilda, you missed the eighth-grade party meeting. I told them your idea about the junk jewelry sale, but they decided to do a raffle instead."

"We could do both," I said, glad to have a problem I could solve quickly for a change. "I'll tell them at the next meeting."

"Gilda, did you bring the birth congratulations card you were going to get for Mrs. Hooper?" Vera, from my art class, stopped to ask.

As I was prying the card from my notebook, Bebe zoomed off and Jane threw herself at me. She hugged me, yelling, "I passed the math test, Gilda. Can you believe it?"

"Told you you could do it," I said. Jane's always expecting to fail tests even though she never has. I spend more time on the phone reassuring her than I do on my own studying.

"Gilda, how come you missed homeroom?" It was Dave, my dearest old friend and the one I unload *my* troubles on. His life is perfect so he doesn't mind.

"Avery again," I said. "I had to police him so he wouldn't cut school."

"Why do you spend so much time on your little brother and sister, Gilda?" Jane asked. She raised her eyebrows at me. "They're your parents' problems. You're still a kid yourself, you know."

I opened my mouth to explain, but she said, "See you guys at lunch," and took off.

"That Jane!" I complained to Dave. "She can run everybody's life but her own."

"Well, she's got a point," Dave said. "You haven't ridden Fettucini in a week because you've had to baby-sit Bliss every day."

It was true. Even though riding Dave's sister's big Appaloosa was still the special treat it had been for me when I first met Dave in fifth grade, I hadn't made time for it. "The thing is, Bliss gets scared if I'm not home with her after school," I said.

"Avery's with her. He's old enough, Gilda. Or your mother could pick her up and take her to the dress shop."

"But Mom wouldn't take Cinder, and Bliss won't go anywhere without her kitten."

"And you always have to be the one to give in?"

"Well, I'm the oldest." Dave didn't understand because he was the youngest by eight years in his family. "Listen," I said, relenting, "maybe today I'll bike over to your place. I can call Bliss and tell her I'll be home a little late."

"Good. Do that." He paused, giving me a serious look, then asked, "So how's it going?" By his tone, I knew he meant with my parents. He was the only friend I'd told about the divorce.

"Dad's getting as mean as Mom," I said. "Now they take turns being nasty to each other."

Dave's features are so fine and regular that he could have been a girl, and when his eyes are full of sympathy the way they were then, he is so gorgeous that I melt. "You want to talk about it?" he asked. "We could go for a walk."

"Leave school?" I loved him for offering to play hooky. He'd never do it for himself, but he'd do it for me if I needed him. "No, that's okay," I said. "I've got to take that earth science test. I'll see you after school."

"Right." He wished me good luck on the test, punched my shoulder lightly, and walked off down the hall. There was no way to tell from his confident, straight-backed stride how shy he is.

A girl I didn't know flashed me an envious look. Everybody thought Dave was my boyfriend. They didn't know he hadn't even kissed me yet. They imagined because we'd been friends since fifth grade that I was set for life, that I'd grow up and marry him or something. And I'm sure they wondered why a boy as good-looking as Dave Curry had picked me. Even my girlfriends only compliment me from the neck up —my wavy black hair or my eyes or my smile. Well, it is a good smile.

My mother's another one who treats my wide hips and big thighs as some kind of birth defect. On our annual pre-school shopping trip, she tried to talk me out of pants and into straight or A-line skirts. I knew she was right, even though I always wear pants. But when I was eyeing some outsized hoop earrings, did she have to say, "And don't even *think* about wearing big jewelry. It'll make you look matronly."

8

Mom looks like a fashion model, but I take after my beefy father. Basically beefy, that's me. It's not much fun in a skinny-loving society. What I do is avoid mirrors, and pretend to be beautiful.

I kept my mind fixed on my work through the dreaded earth science test, which turned out not to be so hard after all. Cheerfully I chugged through math, social studies, and language arts by reminding myself that I was going to ride Fettucini that afternoon. Finally school ended.

The worst thing about November is that it gets dark so early. It was midafternoon, but the heavy gray clouds that followed me as I biked down Rosendale Road to Dave's house made it seem like evening. We both lived in Niskayuna, which is a suburban community outside the old industrial city of Schenectady in upstate New York, but I liked Dave's part of town better than mine. He lived in a big, renovated farmhouse on the Mohawk River.

Fettucini was standing in his paddock. I whistled to him. When he raised his head, wisps of the dry grass he was chewing stuck out comically on either side of his jaw.

"Come on, baby, come to Mama," I called. Fettucini lowered his head, then raised it. Finally he ambled toward mc on his long, knobby legs.

"Hey, Gilda," Dave leaned out from his front porch to yell, "Bliss is on the phone. She wants to know if you're here."

I groaned. "I'll talk to her."

Dave's mother was in the kitchen. As usual, her broad

back was bent over a cookbook. Mrs. Curry spends winters in the kitchen cooking and summers in her beloved garden. "Hi, Gilda, how goes it?" she asked.

"Fine," I said. "What're you going to cook?"

"A nut cake. Want to stay for dinner?"

"Thanks, but I can't today." I picked up the phone.

"It's dark out and you're not home," Bliss said. "You're supposed to be home, Gilda."

"I'm just going to ride Fettucini for a little while, and then I'll be there, Blissy. Avery's home, isn't he?"

"But Avery's mad at me."

"Why? What did you do to him?" It took major mischief to make Avery angry.

"Nothing. It wasn't my fault, Gilda. Please come home, please. You're not supposed to leave me alone. Mom said."

I thought of bribes. I thought of threats. I tried reasoning with her. "Bliss, don't be mean. I've been home with you every afternoon."

"But I need you," Bliss wailed.

It *had* to be the divorce that was making her act so babyish lately. She didn't have any other problems, at least so far as I knew. She sniffled pathetically. "Okay, okay," I said. "I'll come right home."

Dave had Fettucini saddled for me. I kissed the horse's freckled muzzle as he bumped his head against my shoulder affectionately. "You better ride him today, Dave. I've got to go."

He shrugged. "I wish you were *my* sister," he said.

I didn't tell him I liked pretending to be his girlfriend better, because I was afraid it might scare him away.

10

From the drooping yellow branches of the willow tree at the corner of the Currys' property, it's only a couple of miles to my development of small split-level and colonial houses. I pedaled hard and rehearsed another showdown with my parents in my head.

Listen, I'd tell them, *I need to know what your plans are. The kids are hurting. And you may not care about Bliss and Avery, but I do. I'm the one who went to the Halloween parade at the elementary school when neither of you could make it. And I baby-sit Bliss for free, even though other kids get paid for watching their kid brothers and sisters. I even turned down summer camp last year to go to the lake with all of you. That's how important family is to me. So you better understand this divorce isn't just your business. It's ours, and I need to know if and when it's happening.*

While I was at it, I'd make them tell me where we were going to have Thanksgiving this year.

Our house came into view down the road. A few years ago, Dad stained it brown so that he wouldn't have to paint it often. Mom complains that he's lazy about any kind of work that doesn't have to do with tennis. Maybe he is a little. Our house did look shabby compared to the well-kept white houses surrounding it. But gazing at it now, I decided that might be good. I mean, if it was too ugly, nobody would buy it.

Bliss was sitting at the kitchen table cuddling Cinder and crying. The TV screen was lit in the living room, and I saw Avery's bony back up close to it. He was watching a rerun of *Star Trek.* He always sits close, as if he'd like to crawl into the spaceship with his heroes.

11

"Okay, I'm here, Blissy. You can stop crying," I said.

"But Avery yelled at me to get out of the living room," Bliss complained.

"How come he yelled at you?"

"Just because I put Cinder on his back and Cinder scratched him by accident."

"Then it's no big deal. He'll forgive you."

"But I'm mad at him. He *yelled* at me."

"Because you really hurt him," I said.

"*I* didn't. Cinder did."

"But *you* put Cinder on his back, didn't you?" Reasoning with Bliss is a real test of patience.

She pouted. Her pretty, heart-shaped face looked sulky. To distract her I asked her to help me get dinner ready. "It's our night to do it," I said.

"Dad brought home pizza when it was his night. Why don't we have pizza?" Bliss suggested.

"That's only once a week. Tonight we'll have the leftover chicken. We could make it a one-pot meal if we have mushroom soup in the pantry."

"Oh, good. Then Cinder'll get leftovers because Avery hates one-pot meals."

I'd forgotten that. I'd better leave a piece of chicken cold for Avery. "Bliss," I probed, "is anything else bothering you lately? I mean, besides Avery?"

"Well, sort of."

"You're worrying about the divorce, aren't you?" I guessed.

"No," Bliss said. "About a piano. My teacher says I need to practice every day on a piano. But Mom says not to bother her now."

I chucked the big sister reassurance and instead started explaining. "Mom's busy trying to make a go of her business and find an apartment in case somebody buys our house. She can't think about a piano, too, Bliss."

"Where are we going to live if somebody buys our house?" Bliss asked.

"I don't know. But I'll find out soon."

Tonight, I told myself. Tonight, I'd make the parents talk.

2

The big discussion didn't go the way I'd planned it. Dad came home while I was cooking, and said it smelled good but too bad he couldn't stay to eat, that he had to get dressed for a cocktail party.

"A cocktail party?" I said. "I thought you hated those things."

"Yeah, I do, but Pam's got to show up at this one for business reasons."

Pam was his girlfriend. It still jolted me that my father had a girlfriend. "But you don't have to go with her," I said.

"Well, she asked me to, honey. . . . Your mother should be home soon."

"I need to talk to both of you tonight."

"Sounds heavy. I'm glad I won't be here." He poured himself a glass of apple cider and leaned against the sink near where I was working.

Abruptly I asked him, "Dad, do you really want to split with Mom?"

He looked at me in surprise. "Sorry to have to admit it, Gilda, but the truth is I do."

"Then why are you taking so long about it?"

"Well, your mother and I are trying to be as civilized as possible. For your sakes we want this to be a fair and friendly split-up. But as soon as I fix that hole in the basement and shape up the yard, I'll pack and move over to Pam's. . . . Want to come with me? You're welcome, you know, you and Avery and Bliss, too."

"How can we be welcome?" I demanded. "Pam doesn't even know us. And we don't know her."

"Right." He took a long swallow. "But that's easy to fix. We'll have dinner with her. She's got a great house, Gilda — a big old place with lots of space. And it's closer to your school than you are now."

"I don't care about her house. What's *she* like?"

"I tried to tell you, but you didn't want to hear. You'll like her. She's good-looking, like your mother, and hardworking, like your mother, and smart —"

"Like Mom. If she's just like Mom, how come you —"

"Because Pam thinks I'm a neat guy, and your mother thinks I'm a failure." Big as Dad is, his face is as open as a little kid's. I guessed by his hurt look that Mom's mean remarks had gotten to him.

"Pam has a son your age," Dad continued. "Nice kid."

"Does he to go my school?" I was wondering if I knew him.

"No, a private school. He had some learning problem, but he's licked it — just about. Likes tennis."

"That's a switch for you."

Dad grinned. "Yeah, a kid who likes tennis. I've never

had one of those." He finished his cider and walked off to the den, which is his temporary bedroom.

I'm not jealous very often, so it took me a minute to identify what I was feeling. Then I told myself how stupid it was to be jealous of a kid I didn't even know. So what if that boy likes tennis? Dad calls me his first favorite daughter. Unlike Mom, *he* loves me the way I am.

Dad came out in his navy blue suit and tie and asked me what I thought. I said he looked handsome, but really he looked sort of bulgy. His tennis clothes suit him better.

He left, and finally Mom came home. She kicked off her heels and got herself a glass of water at the sink. She always fills herself up with water before dinner so she won't eat too much. "God, what a day," she said. "They sent me the wrong size dress for my best customer, and the saleswoman I just hired didn't show."

"That's too bad," I told her. When she finished recounting her dress shop woes, I said, "Mom, I need to talk to you tonight about what's happening to us. Like where we are going to live and who with."

"With me in my apartment when I find one." She patted my shoulder. "Give me a chance, Gilda. Until we sell the house, we don't have enough money to do anything anyway."

Avery had come into the kitchen and heard us. He said to Mom, "Can I ask a question?"

"Sure." Mom smiled at him. "What's your problem, Av?"

"Will we have to go to the same school after?"

16

"After we move? It depends on where I find a place," Mom said.

"Do you want to change schools?" I asked him, thinking about his unsympathetic teacher.

He shrugged and got that blank look which meant he wasn't going to answer. Bliss came up behind him and plunked herself down at the kitchen table with Cinder. "I don't want to change schools. I like my school," she said.

"I don't want to change either," I put in. "But worst of all is not knowing what's going to happen."

"I'll tell you as soon as I know," Mom said. She lifted the cover of the pot I was monitoring and nodded. "You used up the chicken. Good. Let's eat." Her long red nails clicked against the metal as she set the lid down. She's proud of her nails, but to me they look like claws.

When the four of us were seated around the table eating, I said, "Well, whatever happens, we'll have Thanksgiving together, won't we?"

"How do I know?" Mom snapped. "It's your father who's moving out, not me. I'm sure you'll get to stuff yourself with turkey someplace."

"It's not the turkey I care about, it's being together."

"Must you get so dramatic, Gilda? Thanksgiving's just a holiday where everybody overeats."

"Thanksgiving's a family holiday. You may not care about this family, but I do." I was close to tears. Bliss and Avery were staring at me openmouthedly.

"Don't you try and make me feel guilty," Mom said shrilly. "I get grief enough at work without having you act up at home."

17

"You didn't have to start that dress shop. You could have just gotten a *little* job if you wanted to work."

"A little job? You think that's good enough for your mother? Well, I'm not just your mother, Gilda. I'm a person with lots of ability." Her face was an angry red under her blond hair. She dyed it, but the color looked good on her because her eyes are blue. "I've spent my whole life doing for other people," she went on. "Now I'm doing something for me."

The worst of it was I still hadn't found out anything, even though I'd managed to upset both my parents. I left most of my dinner on my plate and retreated to the bedroom Bliss and I shared.

The next morning everything was normal. Mom clattered down to the dryer in the basement, grumbling to herself about why her favorite half-slip was never clean when she needed it. I locked myself in the bathroom so I could put on some new makeup I'd bought that's supposed to accent my natural beauty without being obvious. Mom named me Gilda after a character in an old movie starring Rita Hayworth. Mom thought Hayworth was gorgeous, and even though I'll never be, every once in a while I try living up to my name. I got one eye accented before Bliss banged on the door.

So much for privacy. I opened the door and my sister cried, "I can't find Cinder, Gilda. She's not in the house anywhere."

"Ask Dad to help you."

"He left already."

"Oh, right, for that lady who can only take tennis

lessons at seven A.M. He probably let Cinder out by mistake. She'll come back, Bliss."

"Noooo!" Bliss wailed.

"I'll help you look in five minutes, okay?"

A long sob, and then I heard Bliss banging on Avery's door and demanding, "Is Cinder in there?" Well, that should wake up Avery if he's gone back to sleep, I thought.

". . . no cats in my world," I heard Avery say.

Next Mom came clacking upstairs still talking to herself. She sounded as if she had on cowboy boots with spurs. I took a swipe with the lip gloss, then went to see what I could do for Bliss.

"Stop fussing about your cat and get dressed," Mom was telling her impatiently. "I'm not driving you to school if you miss the bus." Mom shut herself into her bedroom.

Bliss ran past me sobbing and threw herself facedown on her unmade bed. "Cool it," I said. "I bet Cinder's just hiding." At the risk of ruining the only panty hose I had that fit me, I got down on my hands and knees to look under the beds.

Bliss shut up. For a second the house was quiet, too, except for the distant knocking of the dryer and a faint sound — like a wailing baby, a frantically wailing baby. I got up fast, charged downstairs with Bliss at my heels, and flung open the dryer in the basement.

"Cinder!" Bliss screamed. She grabbed up her cat so fast I couldn't tell if it was hurt. But it *had* managed to leap from the dryer.

"That stupid cat," was all Mom said when Bliss accused her of spin-drying her kitten along with the beige half-slip. Mom examined Cinder and said we didn't need the vet. Except for being a little wobbly, Cinder did seem fine. The half-slip was still wet. Mom decided not to use it.

Bliss went to get dressed. Avery was just starting to put on his sneakers. What a madhouse I lived in! Mom squinted at me speculatively. "You look different this morning," she said. "Are you wearing makeup?"

"Umm," I sort of admitted.

Mom nodded and said, "I like it."

I smiled all the way to the school bus, but before I got on, I remembered my earth science notebook was due today. It was sitting on my desk at home, where I'd finished copying it over at midnight. There was nothing to do but run back and get it, which meant another long bike ride to school on a nasty November day.

Pedaling across the elementary school yard to get to the middle school, I was surprised to see Avery in a huddle of boys next to the windowless back wall of the gym. Usually Avery would be trailing behind a line of kids, or playing off by himself on the playground, or staring at the sky when everyone else was watching a ball game. I'd have to ask him what he was doing with those other sixth-grade boys. It would be great if he'd finally managed to make some friends.

I docked my bike in the rack and raced into school just as the first bell rang.

"You bring your science notebook?" Dave whispered when I sat down next to him in the earth science lab.

"Got it."

"I was thinking," he said, "if things get too complicated, you could always come live with us. My folks think you're a neat kid."

"Thanks." I gave him a fond smile. Even as a brother instead of a boyfriend, he was awesome.

Math was just review work, so I let myself daydream about living at Dave's. Every morning I'd get up and muck out Fettucini's stall and feed him. Then I'd take my time washing up and dressing for school. No cats in dryers to distract me. No anxiety about anybody making it to the school bus. I'd eat the pancakes or oatmeal that Dave told me his mother made alternately for him every morning. I'd listen to Mr. Curry's rundown on the news of the day and agree that the world was in terrible shape. I'd admire Mrs. Curry's elaborate garden and praise her cooking experiments while she told me what a neat kid I was.

After school, Dave and I would exercise Fettucini, and then I'd help get dinner and spend an hour or two on the phone checking up on my family and girlfriends. A little homework, some TV, and then I'd read in bed without worrying about waking up Bliss with the light. It would be like an endless vacation.

I was tempted, but suddenly I was hit with a spasm of love for my own family. How could I leave them to fend for themselves? Dad and Mom might manage without me okay, but not Bliss and Avery.

At lunchtime, I carried my tray to the usual table by the window. Dave was already there. So were my closest girlfriends, Bebe and Jane, and Stephanie and her boyfriend, Mike, who was Dave's Boy Scout buddy. Stephanie was telling one of her dramatic tales about how her parents had walked in on Mike and her when they were arm wrestling and thought there was something sexual going on. Now Steph and Mike weren't allowed to go anywhere alone together.

"Gilda, how about you and Dave going to a movie with us Saturday night?" Stephanie asked.

"I don't know. My life's kind of up in the air right now." I hesitated. Then I thought, I have to tell them sometime, and so I told about the parents' divorce and the house being up for sale. I tried to act as if it were no big deal, but I began to cry, and finally had to admit, "I feel as if I'm free-falling without a parachute."

"Well, join the crowd," Stephanie said. Her mother was on her second divorce. "Nobody says life's going to be easy."

"You like your father best, don't you, Gilda?" Bebe asked thoughtfully. "I mean, you're always battling with your mom. So why don't you work it so that you get to live with your dad? My cousin did that."

"My dad and his *girlfriend*?" I asked. "No thanks."

"My parents are such vegetables. They're so boring," Jane said, as if a divorce were something that might brighten her day.

"Listen, not to worry about the house selling soon anyway," Stephanie said. "Ours was on the market for a year. Meanwhile, my stepfather lost his down payment on the new house. It was a disaster."

"Whatever you do, Gilda," Bebe said with conviction, "you can't leave us."

22

"We need your shoulder to cry on," Jane said.

"You're our resident earth mother," Stephanie said.

"And my best friend," Bebe said.

"Mine, too!" Jane cried.

"Yuck!" Stephanie said, clutching her throat. She hated anything mushy.

When school let out that afternoon, Dave asked, "You coming over?"

"Not today, Dave. But how about Saturday? Bliss can go to the tennis club with Dad then. She likes that."

"Okay, I'll tell Fettucini you're coming."

"Good — and give him a kiss for me."

I rode my bike home the way I'd come, cutting across the elementary school grounds. The buses had left already, but I wasn't surprised to see Avery walking. It's a mile and a half, and he often walked it. In the break between the houses on one hill, you could get a view of the mountains. Avery likes distant views. I wondered if he still dreamed of flying. He used to pretend he could fly. He'd even broken a leg leaping out of a tree to try it when he was four.

"So," I said, stopping my bike next to him. "How goes it?"

"Fine."

"I saw you with a bunch of guys this morning. Friends of yours?"

He looked alarmed. "Not them."

"They weren't giving you a hard time, were they?"

"No."

"So what were you talking to them about?"

23

"Math."

"Oh? They wanted you to help them with their homework or something?"

"Sort of like that."

"Well, you should, Avery. You're smart. Kids'll like you if you can help them out."

"Yeah." He began to move toward home, and I walked my bike along beside him.

Avery's usually talkative, at least alone with me, but he wasn't saying anything that afternoon. "Hey," I said, "you worried about something?"

His owl eyes were trusting. "I did something really bad, Gilda."

"Oh? What?"

"I can't tell you."

A squirrel crossing the road ahead of us narrowly escaped getting hit by a car, but Avery didn't even notice. I said, "Sure you can. You always tell me everything, and I've never given you away, have I?"

"But I can't tell you this, because you won't like it." He folded in his lips as if he thought I might be able to coax the words out of him. "Anyway, I don't have any friends. But if I moved somewhere else, maybe there'd be another kid like me."

"Well, you're special. That's what makes it hard. . . . Did you show your teacher the book you wrote, the one about the Gallyflinkers?"

"Yeah, I showed it to her like you said, and she made me read it to the class during language period."

"Did you wow them?"

He shook his head. "They got bored."

"You didn't try reading them the whole forty-two pages, did you?"

"Yeah, because the first part just describes the Gallyflinkers. Then comes what their planet is like, and then, in chapter three, I do the starship coming from earth with Captain Alvery, but it isn't until chapter four that stuff starts happening. My teacher told them it got better, but kids started yawning and fooling around, and she had to yell at them."

"Did you get to the part where the Gallyflinkers bring Captain Alvery food? That green fluorescent stuff? I loved it when he poisoned himself eating some just so as not to hurt their feelings."

"They didn't listen, Gilda." Avery looked crushed and a nerve jumped in his cheek. He's too sensitive, I thought. He turns pale when he's upset, and his mouth wriggles like a worm on a fishhook. My brother's not a cool kid, definitely not.

Remembering what he'd said before, I told him, "Whatever you did can't have been too bad. Forget it, Av." He doesn't like to be hugged or kissed, but I brushed his hair back from his forehead affectionately. For once, he didn't duck away from me.

"I wrote another chapter," he said. "Want to hear it?"

"Sure. But later. First, before Dad and Mom get home, I want to have a conference with you and Bliss about this divorce business."

"You mean about who we're going to live with? I'm going with Mom if she goes out of the school district."

"You want to get away that bad?" I asked him. "But suppose *I* don't go with Mom?"

"Why wouldn't you?"

"Because of Dave and Fettucini and my friends and — I like it here, Avery."

"Well, then —" He twitched and teetered from foot to foot. "I don't know."

"Listen, Av," I said, "you and Bliss and I have to stick together no matter what. We're like a cell nucleus. Without us, there can't be a family."

"Yeah," Avery agreed. "Only things would be better if I could move."

Bliss wasn't home. I'd forgotten about her music lesson with the lady on the corner.

Somehow I'd have to get my brother and sister alone for a conference after dinner. Maybe nothing much had happened in the months since the parents' divorce announcement, but something told me big changes were about to happen — and I'd better be ready.

3

Mom came home happy for a change. "Good news, girls," she said to Bliss and me as she charged around the kitchen in her stocking feet. She was fixing us what she called "a healthy dinner for a change" — baked white fish, fresh broccoli, and a salad. "I found the right apartment at last."

I stiffened and stopped arguing with Bliss about setting a place at the table for Cinder, who was sitting up in Bliss's lap and eyeing my every move. "An apartment in our school district?" I asked.

"Listen, don't rain on my parade, Gilda," Mom said. "There's nothing in your school district that I can afford. Really. I looked everyplace. And this apartment is near a bus stop, and guess what — there's a swimming pool in the complex. Won't it be great to swim whenever you want next summer?"

"Not if I have to swim alone," I said. "Summer is when I have the time to get together with my friends."

"I'm sure you'll find kids your age in the complex,

and the pool's the place to meet them." Mom's eyes brightened as she added, "The kitchen has a dishwasher *and* a disposal. And there are lots of windows. The only drawback is I had to take a one-bedroom apartment. They didn't have a two-bedroom available. But that's just as well, because I can't afford one yet anyway."

Mom held up her hand as I opened my mouth to protest. "Don't worry. We'll upgrade to two bedrooms the minute my business expands."

"But we can't all fit into one bedroom," I pointed out.

"Well, it'll be tight." Mom shrugged. "But so what? When I was a kid we slept three to a room. If I could manage, so can you. I figure you'll sleep with me, and Bliss can have the couch in the living room, and Avery'll make do with a sleeping bag on the floor. He usually ends up on the floor anyway, don't you, Av?"

"Sometimes. . . . There's more room on the floor," Avery said. He'd appeared in the kitchen a minute after *Star Trek* ended.

Cautiously, so as not to make Mom explode, I asked her, "Why not keep looking for a place in this school district — until the house sells anyway?"

"Oh, didn't I tell you?" Mom said — casually, as if she didn't know she was dropping a bomb. "We finally got an offer. That old couple two houses down has a married daughter who wants to move into this neighborhood."

"You're kidding!" I shrieked. "The house is sold?"

"Well, almost. It's the only bid we've had, and we'd be nuts not to take it, considering the market."

28

Hearing that made me so angry that I was the one who exploded. "Who'd be nuts not to take it? There's no 'we' in this. It's all you. *You're* the one who wants to move. *You* get what you want, and we lose our friends and our home and everything we've known all our lives."

"Gilda, spare me the melodrama! I'm not ruining your lives by squeezing you into a small apartment for a few months. And other kids change schools all the time. You're just lucky you've never had to. In fact, this will be good experience for all three of you."

"Not for me, it won't," I protested.

"Well, Avery's glad to change schools, aren't you, Av?" Mom asked. Avery slid a guilty look at me, but he nodded. "And Bliss doesn't mind, do you, baby?"

"Uh-uh," Bliss said. "Cinder and me can sleep anywhere. But, Mom, can I have a piano?"

Mom rolled her big blue eyes. "If we squeezed a piano into this place, there wouldn't be room for us. Think small, Bliss, small."

I couldn't believe it. My own brother and sister betrayed me. It was too much. I ran upstairs and threw myself down on my bed. For months, we'd been teetering on the edge of a cliff, and now we were falling. I felt desperate. Dad, Dave, my friends, my school, my house since I was two — all had to be left behind. And what was Mom offering us in exchange? A swimming pool for hot summer days. How could she do this to me?

Bliss tiptoed into the bedroom, still toting Cinder. She sat down next to me and patted my arm. Then she hugged me. "Want to hear my ballet music tape?" I'd told her it was my favorite.

"Yes, please," I said, grateful that somebody wanted to comfort me. I lay there scratching Cinder behind her ears and let the music glide over me while I stared at Bliss's cat pictures.

Half the room was Bliss's, so half the room was decorated with images of cats. Black cutouts of cats climbed around the top corners of the window. A big poster of the three little kittens hung over Bliss's bed, and a moody Siamese was framed on the wall next to the closet. Stuffed cats filled the top shelf of the bookcase. At one time, when Bliss was five or six, she'd answered "meow" instead of yes to questions, and Mom had wondered aloud if she was normal.

"Of course she is," I'd assured Mom. "Bliss'd just rather be a cat than a kid."

Grandma from New York had been visiting at the time. She'd gotten Mom's back up by saying that it was normal not to want to be a child in our house. "Avery wants to be a robot; Bliss wants to be a cat; and Gilda wants to be an adult," Grandma had said. That had been before Avery fixed on space travel and being captain of a starship.

I hadn't realized how much I wanted to be grown up until Grandma said that about me. She's Dad's mother, our only remaining grandparent. Mom's mother died long ago. I never knew her, because Mom didn't keep up with her family. She said they were always measuring things, like who was best-looking or smartest or had the most money. And Mom always came up short.

Grandma was right about my not wanting to be a child. I don't know why I'm so impatient to grow up. I guess I like responsibility and I want to decide things myself. I hate having to accept what adults think is good for me, even if it is, even if the adults are parents who love me. I don't want to be a chess piece. I want to be the player.

"Bliss, we need to talk," I said now, and I sat up with new energy. "We need to decide where we're going to live."

"I want to live here."

"Sure, but you can't. You heard Mom. The house sold. We have to move. Now, you have a choice — Mom, or Dad and his girlfriend. If we go with Mom, we lose our friends and get squeezed. If we go with Dad, we get his girlfriend and her kid. . . . I think she has a big house, though."

Bliss frowned, thinking. "I don't care so long as Cinder comes. You choose, Gilda."

"Bliss," I asked out of curiosity, "tell me something. What would you do if the house were burning and you could only save me or Cinder?"

"Save Cinder," Bliss said promptly. "You're a big girl, Gilda. You could get out by yourself."

I had to laugh. She was so practical. "Some sister you are," I teased.

"Why do we have to get divorced, Gilda?" she asked suddenly. "Why can't we just stay like we are?"

Now it was my turn to do the comforting. I rocked Bliss in my arms. "Maybe Dad's girlfriend will turn out to be a music teacher or something. Maybe she'll have a piano."

Later I cornered Dad in the garage as he was getting out of his car. "Did you know the house has been sold?" I asked, folding my arms across my chest.

"I heard a neighbor made an offer. Your mother called me at work. You're upset, huh, honey?"

"And Mom's found an apartment — out of the school district. She wants Avery to sleep on the floor."

"Yeah, well, I told you —" Dad slammed his door shut "— any or all of you guys are welcome at Pam's house. I talk about you so much she says she feels as if she knows you already. Pam likes kids."

There was no way he could duck out of this conversation with both me and a wall of junk blocking his way. I stood my ground. "You said we'd get to meet her."

"Right. I'll call and ask her when she's free."

"Couldn't we just go to her house tonight and sit down and talk?"

"What's the rush? You can't get to know her in one evening anyway."

"If she likes kids so much, how come she only had one?"

"Because she got divorced," Dad said. "You'll like her, Gilda. She's a great gal." He put his hands on my shoulders. "Now move, will you?"

"Well, make it soon, Dad. Tell her it's urgent."

"You bet. Will do." He grinned at me. "You're my first favorite daughter, you know."

"I know, Dad. I love you, too." I kissed him and led the way to the kitchen. All things being equal, I'd be happier living with him than with Mom. Avery wouldn't get to change schools, but maybe I could help him with whatever problem he was having at his school. Yes, it would work out better this way. As for Mom, she'd probably be relieved to have us off her back.

After dinner, Dad returned to the living room from a phone conversation in the kitchen to announce we were all invited to Pam's for dinner Friday night. "Mom, too?" Bliss asked.

"Your mother goes back to work Friday evenings," Dad said. He looked at Mom who was sitting on the couch sewing a button on Bliss's jumper, which Bliss was still wearing.

"I don't think your father's girlfriend's too interested in entertaining me, Blissy," Mom said with a smirk and a raised eyebrow.

"But if she's going to be our mother too . . ." Bliss said. She looked so cute as she puzzled things out. "Like you wanted to meet the baby-sitter you left us with when you and Dad went away."

"Who says Pam's going to be your mother?" Mom demanded.

"Well, if we're going to live with her like Gilda says," Bliss said, "that sort of makes her like a —"

"You're *my* children," Mom yelled. She turned on me, her hawk eyes blazing. "Now what are you plotting? Why are you always trying to turn your brother and sister against me, Gilda?"

"I'm not," I said. "Anyway, you're the one who's breaking up our family."

"Me? Just me? What about your father? He found himself a girlfriend quick enough the minute we decided to get divorced, didn't he?"

"I'm mad at both of you," I said. "You didn't even go for counseling. I thought people were supposed to go for counseling before they got divorced." I was so upset I was shaking.

"Gilda," Dad said. "We did that. We went for over a year."

"And you didn't tell us?" I'd thought at least I knew what was going on in my own family. Now I find out they were keeping secrets from me as if I were the enemy. I got up from Dad's club chair and began pacing the room, passing Avery, who was nose to nose with the TV as usual.

"We didn't want to worry you," Mom said. "Listen, Gilda, you've always complained that we fight too much. You ought to be glad we won't be fighting anymore."

"I'd rather have you fighting than getting divorced," I said. "At least you can make up from a fight and stay together."

"Listen," Mom tried again, "we've stuck it out for thirteen years for your sake. Now it's our turn. If I wait till you grow up, it'll be too late for me. I'm thirty-one already."

I knew how old Mom was. I knew she'd had me soon after her eighteenth birthday. Suddenly I knew something else — something that chilled me. But I shoved the idea back to be considered later. "Then why did you have Avery and Bliss?" I asked Mom.

Dad groaned and covered his face. Mom kept her cool. "Because your father wanted me to keep having babies. He *likes* babies."

"That's not fair," Dad said. "I never had to work very hard to persuade you."

"Sure. You could sweet-talk me into anything in those days," Mom said. "But I'm not the fool kid I was."

"No, you're the mother of three now," I pointed out.

Avery turned his pale bewildered face my way. I guessed he was listening to the family fight rather than the TV, but he was letting me be the spokesman as usual. Bliss's button was back in place, but she hadn't left the couch. She was hunched over, squeezing Cinder so hard that the kitten was meowing pitifully.

"I know I'm a mother. Believe me, I know it," Mom said. "None of you can complain about being neglected. I do my jobs well — all of them."

Suddenly Cinder yowled and leaped from Bliss's arms. Bliss began to cry.

"That's enough now," Mom said when I opened my mouth again. "If you think living with your father's girlfriend would be so great, then go. But if you change your mind, I'll be waiting for you, Gilda."

I'd hurt Mom's feelings. I knew I should apologize, but I was too angry. We'd meet Pam — Bliss and Avery and I — and then we'd see where we'd be better off living.

I went out to the backyard to get a breath of fresh air. A crescent moon was lying in a nest of clouds. The thought I'd held off before came back to me now as cold as the night air around me. Mom must have gotten pregnant by mistake with me while she was still a teenager. I was the reason she and Dad had been stuck with each other all these years. It was my fault for being born.

Friday morning my friend, the middle-school librarian, told me that Avery was in serious trouble. His math teacher had told her that Avery had stolen the math teacher's computer code and copied the answers to the unit tests for the year. That must be the bad thing he couldn't tell me.

At lunchtime, I left the middle school without permission and raced over to the elementary school. Avery was sitting on the bench in the office looking white-faced and miserable. The secretary recognized me. "How's it going, Gilda? You in high school now?"

"Next fall," I said, and chatted with her for a minute. Finally I asked Avery if he'd seen the principal yet.

"Yeah, he saw me."

"Well, how come you're still here?"

"He said I had to stay until I told him."

"Told him what?"

"Why I did it."

"So why did you do it? You always get great marks in math."

"I can't tell you."

"It was those boys, wasn't it?"

He looked at me fearfully. "Shhh," he said.

"What did they say they'd do to you?"

He pressed his lips shut. His eyelids twitched.

"Avery, you can tell me. I'm your sister."

I could feel him withdrawing from me. He had always been able to hole up inside himself and stay there indefinitely, as if he could put himself into a state of suspended animation — as if he really were a space traveler. I left him and managed to get back into the middle school without being discovered.

As soon as the last bell rang, I returned to the elementary school to see what had happened to my brother. Avery was gone from the office. The secretary said the principal had dismissed him. "Your father's coming in with him tomorrow morning," she said.

"Can I speak to Mr. Hammer?"

"I'll see." Obligingly the secretary went to the door of the principal's office and said, "Gilda wants to talk to you. Avery's sister?"

"He didn't do it for himself," I told Mr. Hammer. "Math's his best subject. He got bullied into it."

"I suspect you're right, Gilda. But until Avery tells me who the other kids are, I've got no one else to blame. Stealing a teacher's code is serious stuff."

"He'll never tell on them. He won't. I know my brother." I looked straight at Mr. Hammer. "Then what are you going to do to him?"

"Don't worry. He'll tell. You leave it to your father and me, okay?"

I worried all the way home. Avery was so sensitive. When he started first grade, he'd awakened us for months with his nightmares. Spend more time with him, the pediatrician had advised. So Dad had tried to get Avery interested in tennis, had even taken him fishing, but nothing helped.

Mom had threatened, "Avery, if you don't stop acting so spacey, you'll wind up in a school for the emotionally disturbed. You want to go to a special school with weird kids?"

"No," Avery had said. He had, for a while then, made an effort to tune in to the world around him. He had begun writing his stories and sharing them with me.

"Do you think I'm weird?" he'd asked me one day after kids had mocked him on the playground.

"Of course not. You just spend more time thinking than most kids," I'd said. "You should do what other kids do, Av. Play kickball . . . or how about Nintendo?"

Last year Mom got a used Nintendo game for Avery from a friend of hers. As long as it was working, a new boy in his class came home with Avery every day to play Nintendo. He stopped coming, though, after the game broke down.

Dad had talked about getting it fixed or buying a new one.

"That's okay," Avery had said. "I'm kind of tired of it anyway."

"What about your friend? You could invite him over to play something else," I had suggested.

"No. He doesn't really like me."

"How do you know?"

"Well, in school, he acts like he doesn't know me. See, he's afraid the other kids'll make fun of him and, you know, call him names like they do me."

"I'll go talk to your teacher," I said.

"No, don't," Avery said. "It doesn't matter. I don't listen to what those kids say."

Dad had suggested karate lessons, but Avery said he didn't want any more classes in anything.

Mom teased, "Avery doesn't think he needs to get along with other people. He thinks any minute a spaceship's going to land in the backyard and take him away to where he belongs. Right, Avery? If a spaceship landed and little green men got out, you'd go with them, wouldn't you?"

Avery had looked at her in misery with pinched nostrils and a twitching mouth, but he didn't defend himself.

"That's not funny, Tina," Dad had said.

"How did I get these kids anyway?" Mom complained. "Not one of them's like me."

"Bliss looks just like you," I had said.

"Yeah, but she doesn't care how she looks. Cats and music, that's all Bliss cares about."

"Gilda's a regular kid. She's our all-American girl," Dad had said.

Mom's eyebrow shot up, and she didn't smile when she told him, "Gilda's yours. You're the original all-American boy, aren't you?"

What would Mom think about Avery stealing the

math teacher's code? Would she take it as seriously as the principal did? What if she decided Avery really needed a special school? But there was nothing wrong with my brother. The things he imagined were just more interesting than the world around him.

He needed a friend, that's what he needed. And maybe he was right — maybe he'd have a better chance of finding one if he were living with Mom and going to a different school.

For the first time, I considered letting my brother go.

4

Pam lived in the old part of town where every house looked as if it had been built to show how important its owners were. Her house towered over two giant trees and made the church across the street look small. "What does she do with all that *space*?" I asked Dad. "Does she rent rooms?"

Dad got out of the car and stood beside me, looking up at the house. "Well, this was her parents' place. Nice, huh?"

"She must be rich," Avery said. He hadn't budged from the back seat where he was sitting beside Bliss. She hadn't moved either.

"I bet Cinder would have fun exploring this house," I said to Bliss, who looked a little scared.

"She'd get lost," Bliss said.

"No way," Dad said. "You think Cinder's a dummy? Come on. Get out of the car."

Avery eased himself onto the sidewalk reluctantly, but Bliss said, "I'm not very hungry," and stayed put.

"Come on, baby doll. You don't want to embarrass me, do you?" Dad asked.

"Don't you want to see what's inside the house?" I coaxed. "Who knows? Pam may even have cats, Blissy."

Sighing, Bliss got out of the car, but she grabbed hold of my hand.

Pam was taller than Mom, and brown-haired rather than blond, but she had the same cool, confident look. Like Mom, she had high arched eyebrows and a tooth-paste-ad smile. She was wearing a tailored wool dress. I was glad I'd dressed up in a skirt and my best blouse and had washed my hair. "You've got an interesting house," I said.

"Thank you." Pam looked pleased. "I'm kind of partial to the place. Would you like a tour before we sit down?"

"Sure. That'd be fun," I said. Bliss and Avery fell into line behind me. With Pam in the lead and Dad trailing us, we went from the square entry hall to the enormous living room, which had a lot of comfortable-looking upholstered furniture near a white paneled fireplace. In the back was a library's worth of bookcases, also a television. I enthused about everything, especially the high ceilings and the paneled fireplace.

"I grew up in this house," Pam said. "You just don't get architectural details like these in modern homes. Look at this woodwork, for instance."

We were in the hall. I admired the fancy woodwork around the doorways and the stairs, and then we went to a kitchen that stretched across the whole back of the house. "Wow! Who cleans this?" I asked.

Pam laughed. "You're too young to wonder about things like that, Gilda." She told me she had a woman come in to clean once a week. "Pauli and I don't make much mess anyway," Pam said. "He mostly hangs out in his room, and I'm pretty neat."

"Is he home?" I asked.

"Yes. He'll be down later. He's not very social, I'm afraid."

"Avery's not social either," I said to prod him into joining the conversation. "Maybe you and Pauli have something in common, Av."

Avery ducked his head and mumbled a question that Pam had to ask him to repeat. "Is it okay if I watch my show on your TV?"

"Sure. *Star Trek*, right? Your father told me. We'll hold dinner until it's over."

Avery thanked her and left for the living room.

"Do you like cats?" Bliss suddenly asked Pam.

"Well, I would, except I'm allergic to them. I get all the symptoms of a bad cold if I get within ten feet of a cat."

"I didn't know that," Dad said.

"Just because we've known each other forever doesn't mean we don't have a lot to learn about each other," Pam said. She smiled at me. "Did your dad tell you we met way back in college days? I was trying out for the tennis team, and your father used to come to hit with me. I kept bugging him to try out for the team, too, because he was a much better player than I was, but he said he didn't have the time."

"Well, I didn't," Dad said quickly. "I was tending bar

nights and going to college days, and in between I was helping your mother out with you, Gilda." He gave me a smile.

"We lost track of each other after your father dropped out of college," Pam said. "It was a real surprise to bump into him at the tennis club."

"Oh, is that where you met?" Of course, it had to be the tennis club, because where else did Dad ever go alone?

Pam showed us the room-sized pantry and the formal dining room with its crystal chandelier over a big polished wood table. The drapes matched the wallpaper in a flowery pattern of rose and white. "It's really pretty," I said. I was wondering if Dad would have married Pam back then if he hadn't already been married. It was hard to imagine Pam being my mother. But then I wouldn't have been me if she had been Dad's wife. I became me because Mom was my mother — but what was there of Mom in me? I didn't see myself as being like her at all, except maybe that I liked to work.

"Your father tells me you're a people person," Pam said to me as she led us up the stairs.

"Yes, I like people."

"And they like you, I bet," Pam said.

"I'm a cat person," Bliss offered.

"Definitely," I said.

"This house is so big, you could keep a cat here, and it would stay far, far away from you — if you wanted it to," Bliss said.

"The trouble is cats don't stay put very well," Pam said. She stopped on the second-floor landing, where there were more bookshelves and a table with a vase of fresh flowers on it.

"You could get shots," Bliss said.

"She means the kind that desensitize you," I explained.

"Fortunately I don't have to," Pam said. "I'm fine as long as I keep away from furry felines. Besides, if I were going to get shots, it would be so that we could have a dog. I love dogs, but Pauli doesn't want to be stuck walking one all the time, and I'm not home much. . . . That's Pauli's room." She pointed to a closed door as she walked us down a long, wide hall.

"The top floor's mostly unused," Pam said. "Not worth looking at."

But it didn't matter how much room Pam had, I was thinking. If Cinder wasn't welcome, Bliss wouldn't come. Too bad, because so far I liked Pam and her house.

She served us a chicken dinner with a big salad and rice and snow peas. "Everything looks delicious," I said, and offered to help bring things to the table.

"Just relax, Gilda. It's all organized," Pam told me.

Well, Mom was efficient, too, I thought. What did Dad need another wife for if she was just a duplicate of his first one? Except Pam was rich, and Dad had come from a rich family. He'd been raised in Grandma's apartment on Fifth Avenue in New York City and sent to private schools. Maybe that gave him more in common with Pam than with Mom.

I checked on my brother and sister. Bliss was eating her dinner. Avery was picking at his. Pauli's plate was full, but he hadn't appeared even though his mother had called him.

"Do you like being a stockbroker?" I asked Pam to make conversation.

"I love it. Something's happening all the time, and I enjoy the challenge of keeping up when the pace gets hectic."

"What's more," Dad said, "Pam still plays a mean game of tennis, and she skis. This winter I'm going to buy myself a new pair of skis and see if I remember how to navigate a slope. You kids want to come along?"

"Not me," Bliss blurted out just as I said, "Sure, that'd be fun." To my surprise, Avery looked up and said he'd like to learn to ski.

"Good," Pam said. "Pauli's a skier, too. We can all go together."

At that moment, a tall, strongly built boy who looked a lot like Pam slipped into his seat at the table. He mumbled a "hi" and began eating his dinner. I couldn't see his face too well because it was bent over the cooling food on his plate.

"So there you are, Pauli," Pam said. When she introduced him to us, he stopped forking food into his mouth and nodded, but he didn't look at us.

Suddenly Avery knocked over his long-stemmed water glass. "Sorry. Gee, I'm sorry." He looked horrified. Pauli laughed.

"Pauli, that's not funny," Pam said as she picked up the glass.

"It is when someone else does it," Pauli said.

"Glasses rarely stay upright very long at our dinner table," Pam confessed.

"Do you like going to a private school, Pauli?" I asked to get him talking.

"No."

"Oh. Then why do you go?"

"Mom made me because I couldn't read good — well — but now I can read okay, and she still won't —"

"That'll do, Pauli," Pam said. "Cool it."

He shut up and began eating again. I felt a little sorry for him. Pam was tough — like Mom. Maybe even tougher.

"Now what were we talking about?" Pam said.

"I don't know," Dad said. "Pauli may be a little klutzy at the dinner table, but he's plenty agile on the tennis court. He's got a natural top spin and a promising serve."

"Do you play tennis too, Avery?" Pam asked.

He smiled shyly at her and said, "I'm no good at it."

"None of us are," I said. The water had made a large wet stain on the white tablecloth. I was trying to blot it up with my cloth napkin. Bliss leaned across to try to help and managed to knock over my water glass as well.

"Oops," Bliss said, and she looked guiltily at Pam.

Pam laughed. "Good thing it's water and not wine. Don't worry, girls. The pads will protect the table-top."

Tough but nice, I decided. If only Pam weren't allergic to cats.

"Does the school Pauli goes to cost a lot?" Avery asked abruptly.

"Avery!" I said.

"Were you thinking of changing schools, Avery?" Pam asked.

"I need to," he said.

"Avery got suspended," Dad explained, "and he's not allowed back unless he names names." Dad was shifting his eyebrows up and down as if he thought the situation were somehow humorous.

Mom hadn't thought it was humorous. When Dad came home with Avery from the principal's office that afternoon and told Mom about the suspension, she had been furious. She had screamed that it would be bad for Avery to be left home alone all day, that he needed the reality of school and having to do things he didn't want to do, and that getting in trouble certainly wasn't funny.

"You get him to tell who put him up to stealing the teacher's code then," Dad had told Mom. "I couldn't budge him."

"Gilda," Mom had said, "talk to your brother."

"Sorry," I had said. "He won't even tell me."

Finally Mom had thrown up her hands and gone after Avery herself, but she hadn't made him talk.

All he'd say about the whole thing was that he was sorry.

"It doesn't seem fair," Pam was saying when I tuned back in to the conversation at the table about Avery's suspension. "Can't you do something about it, Skip?"

"No need," Dad said. "Eventually the principal has

to take Av back. A kid can't be kept out of school indefinitely."

"I don't want to go back," Avery said.

"You'll have to, Avery," Dad said. "Unfortunately, I
can't afford the kind of private school Pauli goes to."

"Oh," Avery said. Then he muttered, "That's okay,"
and ducked his head.

The only one of us who would want to move to Pam's
house was me, it seemed. That was discouraging.

After eating ice cream and cookies for dessert, I offered to help Pam with the dishes. "I appreciate the
offer," she said, "but I'd rather do them later and enjoy
my company."

She put her hand on my shoulder as we stood in the
foyer to say good-bye. "Your father's very proud of
you," she said, "and I can see why. You're a very mature
girl, Gilda."

I glanced at Dad to see if he had heard the compliment. He was grinning. "Well, Avery and Bliss are good
kids, too," I said. "Actually, they're better than me in
some ways. They don't talk back, and I do. I fight with
my mom all the time."

"Do you really?" Pam didn't sound as if she thought
that was so terrible.

"Gilda's great, but she does like to run the show,"
Dad said.

I frowned at him. He didn't have to be that truthful
about me in front of a stranger. "That's because I'm the
only one around to take charge lately," I threw back at
him.

"Uh-oh. It's time we got out of here," Dad said. He

waved at Pauli, who was heading upstairs. "See you at the club for your lesson, Pauli."

"Right. Nice meeting you guys," Pauli said, still climbing.

"Are you going to live in that house, Daddy?" Bliss asked when we were settled back in the car.

"Yes, honey. Pam and I plan to get married."

"Well, but I can't live there," Bliss said.

"Why not?" Dad asked.

"Because she won't let Cinder come," Bliss said.

"You and Gilda and I can move with Mom," Avery said.

"Thanks a lot," Dad said. "What about me? Who's coming with me?"

I patted his arm. "We'll see, Dad." But I was already resigning myself to moving to Mom's one-bedroom apartment. What I could do was let Bliss sleep with Mom, and I'd sleep in the living room with Avery. He and I could alternate who got the pullout bed and who got the floor.

"So what did you think of Pam?" Dad asked me, when we were back home and Avery and Bliss had gone upstairs to get ready for bed.

"I liked her."

"Listen," Dad said, "it might be good for you to move in with Pam and me and leave your mother to deal with Avery and Bliss. You'd have your own room, and the way Pam runs a house, it'd be easier for you."

"I don't want to be separated from Bliss and Avery."

"You're not their mother, Gilda. They're too dependent on you. Let them learn to stand on their own."

"We'll see," I said again.

Mom wasn't home yet. Dad went to the living room to watch TV. I called Dave, glad for the chance of a private chat with him.

"Well, how did it go?" he asked.

I gave him my bad-news headlines all at once. "No cats. Pam's allergic."

"Uh-oh, that settles that. Do you want me to ask my parents if they'll take in the three of you? I know they won't mind Cinder."

"Well, it won't hurt to ask," I said. But I suspected neither of my parents would allow us to go live with strangers. In her heart, Mom might want to be free of us, but she also thought of herself as a good mother, and Dad certainly wanted to be a good father.

"I'll be over to ride Fettucini early, Dave," I said. "Then I'll come home and do a little raking for Dad. He promised to get the leaves off the lawn for the new owners."

"I'll mow it for you," Dave said. "That'll take care of the leaves."

"No, thanks. I can use the mower if I get tired of raking."

"Yeah, but last time you messed up on the corners," Dave reminded me.

"So what, it's just grass."

"You made it look like ocean waves."

"New style?" I tried.

"Grass is supposed to be neat. Neat's not your thing, Gilda."

"Thanks a bunch. Who needs a friend like you?"

"Why? You want to be perfect?"

"Dave, my life's getting more fouled up every day," I said suddenly.

"You feeling bad?"

"You try getting divorced and see how good you feel."

"I can imagine," he said.

He couldn't, but I felt guilty for giving him a hard time. I apologized and told him I'd see him in the morning.

A minute after I hung up, Grandma phoned. Dad answered. Normally Grandma kept her long-distance calls down to five minutes or less. People need a lot of money to live like she does in a big apartment with a doorman on Fifth Avenue across from Central Park, but Grandma doesn't like to spend. For Christmas and birthdays, when she asks Dad what the children want, she means what do we want that costs under twenty dollars. But that evening she must have had a lot to say. Suddenly Dad called, "Gilda, your grandma wants to talk to you."

"To me?" I sighed. Usually when my grandmother wanted to talk to me, it was about what she thought we were doing wrong. Hair is a big item for Grandma. She likes it short and neat. She'd say she didn't understand why Mother never took me for a haircut.

"Because Gilda would have a fit if I did," Mom had snapped once. It's true. I need my long hair to balance my big body. Grandma didn't like my body either. Last Christmas she offered to pay for me to go to Weight Watchers, a more-than-twenty-dollar gift, which meant Grandma thought it was important.

"I'm not fat," I told her indignantly. "I'm just big boned like Dad."

"Your father could use Weight Watchers too," Grandma had said. She was thin herself, but then she ate very little, a soft-boiled egg for breakfast, a half-cup of cottage cheese and fruit for lunch, and three ounces of protein and a vegetable for dinner. I knew, because Mom had left the feeding of Grandma to me on her annual Christmas visits.

I also knew that Grandma sneaked chocolates between meals.

"Hi, Grandma, how are you?" I held the phone as if it might bite.

"How should I be when my son's family is breaking apart?"

My throat tightened. Dad must have told her the house had been sold and the divorce was going through.

"Well, what's your opinion of this mess?" Grandma asked.

"My opinion?" I was amazed at the question.

"As the only sensible person there, yours is the opinion I rely on. Do you think their marriage can be saved?"

"I don't know. Mom's gung ho on having her own business, and Dad's already got a pretty neat girlfriend lined up as his next wife."

"He says I will actually approve of this 'girlfriend'

of his. He says she's a very impressive, intelligent woman."

"I guess so."

"I offered to come up to help you," Grandma said. "It's a difficult time for you children. But your father told me he didn't think it would be wise."

I was rapidly weighing the pros and cons of Grandma's interference. Offhand, it came out heavy on the cons. She and Mom just don't get along. "Our big problem is Bliss's cat," I remarked for something to say. "If Pam — that's Dad's girlfriend — weren't allergic to cats, we could all move in with her and leave Mom to do her thing, and we wouldn't have to change schools or anything, but being as Pam's allergic, Bliss doesn't want to go to her house."

"My poor grandchild!" Grandma said in a sympathetic voice.

"Me?" I asked.

"Bliss. That dear child needs a stable environment."

"Umm. We all do."

I was about to describe Avery's predicament, but Grandma said, "At least you're strong, Gilda. As for your brother, he's off in his own world anyway. But Bliss — well, let me think about it."

She barely gave me time to return her "good-bye" before she hung up. No "I love you" of course. Grandma's not much on I-love-yous. I could have used one. Instead I had to be satisfied with being told I was strong and sensible. Well, those were more compliments than I could ever remember getting from her before.

Telling myself nothing final had happened yet, I walked up the stairs to my room. I still hoped Mom and Dad might decide they loved each other after all. I still hoped I was just having a bad dream. If I wasn't, I was probably going to wind up sleeping in Mom's living room with Avery.

5

I woke to the toasty vanilla smell of Mom's fluffy French toast. No one makes it better. She uses an uncut loaf of a special kind of egg bread from the bakery, and slices the pieces thick so they soak up the egg and milk mix and come out crisp outside and soft in the middle. Making French toast is Mom's way of showing she loves us.

I pulled on my jeans and got a glimpse of my lower half in Bliss's mirror. Ugh. Why did everybody else in the whole world get to be narrow and me so broad? Except for Mrs. Curry. Even as a girl she must have been big, and Mr. Curry had married her anyway. Think beautiful, I told myself and hurried downstairs.

Mom was at the stove. I hugged her and said, "Umm, that smells good!"

"Go sit down, Gilda. I know you only love me for my French toast," Mom said. I sat.

Bliss and Avery were already eating. Dad, who didn't like sweet things for breakfast, was leaning against the kitchen counter, forking up leftovers from a plastic container. We made a TV-perfect family scene, except that Avery was crouched under the table with his toast.

"What're you doing under there?" I asked.

"He's mad at us," Mom said.

"Not at Dad, just at you," Avery said from under the table.

"I just want to know why you did it," Mom said. "Just explain to me why."

"He told you he doesn't know," Dad said. "Why won't you accept that?"

"Because when a kid who's never stolen anything steals something, there's got to be a reason," Mom said.

"It's no big deal," Dad said. "He's not beginning a life of crime."

"How do you know? Maybe next time he'll stick up a gas station," Mom said.

"You're making too big a thing of it," Dad said.

"Getting suspended from school *is* a big thing, especially since he can't go back until he tells who got him to do it," Mom said. "What if your son never graduates from elementary school? You want him to spend the rest of his life under a table?" Mom flipped a piece of toast and slapped it into the pan for emphasis.

"You planning to tell or not?" Dad asked Avery.

"Not," came his voice from under the table.

"Do you want another piece of toast, Avery?" Mom asked him.

"*I* want one," I said. "Please."

"Yours is coming," Mom said.

Bliss swallowed her last bite of toast and said,

"Gilda, I've been calling and calling and Cinder doesn't come. Please help me find her."

"She'll come when she's ready," I said. "If she's not here by the time I get back from riding Fettucini, I'll help you then, Blissy."

"Today you all have to start packing," Mom announced. "Not your clothes yet, but whatever else you really want to keep. Separate what we can give away or send to the dump." She gave us each a stare that meant *this means you,* and continued, "Moving day's a week away, and I want to start carting stuff to the apartment a few boxes at a time."

It got my back up that Mom was so sure we were all going with her. "What about my furniture?" I asked.

"No room for it. We'll put it in the garage sale, and I'll give you half of whatever we get," Mom said. "Fair enough?"

"No. That furniture took me most of last summer to sand and paint. I love it and I want to keep it."

"Find someone to store it for you then," Mom said. "My apartment can't hold more than my bedroom set, the living room and kitchen furniture, plus our clothes. And the clothes may have to stay in boxes. The closet space isn't that great."

"Pam's got plenty of room for you, Gilda," Dad said.

Mom smacked her hand on the counter. "What are you trying to do, bribe her?"

"Yes," Dad said with a grin.

"Gilda, you promised we'd be together," Bliss said. "Me and Avery need you."

I got a painful knot in my chest. This family! Why

did I love them when they were so impossible? Avery tapped my leg. "You could send your bedroom to Pam's house and you could come with us to Mom's," he said.

"Good idea," Mom said. Now it was her turn to smile.

"Forget that," Dad said. "I'm not insulting Pam by using her house as a storage facility. Any kid who wants to move in is welcome, but not just furniture."

Suddenly I was fed up with all of them. I stood up and said, "Fettucini's waiting for me. 'Bye, all."

"I haven't finished making your toast yet," Mom said.

"And you have to help me find Cinder," Bliss cried.

"Maybe he's locked in a closet. Like that other time, remember?" I said.

Bliss nodded. "Wait for me. I'll go upstairs and look."

"I thought you liked Pam and her house," Dad said to me.

"I do, but . . . Dad, Bliss and Avery and I have to stick together, or there won't be any family left. And Bliss won't go to Pam's house if she can't take Cinder. We've got to go to Mom's place."

"Gee, thanks," Mom said. "I'm overwhelmed by your enthusiasm for life with your mother."

"Mom, don't pretend it matters so much to you," I said. "You really don't care if I come or not."

"Who says? It's not my fault we fight. When you turned out to be a girl, I thought we'd be good friends."

I couldn't believe it. She'd never acted as if she wanted to be my friend. I looked at her, standing there with her spatula raised and her eyes hurt and accusing, and I felt confused. "But you wouldn't have picked such a little apartment if you really wanted us with you," I

59

said. "I mean, you could have found more space in some big old house somewhere — couldn't you've?"

"I don't want to live in an old house," Mom yelled. "I won't settle for tacky. I put up with leaky toilets and roaches long enough when I was a kid!" She threw the spatula into the sink and stalked out of the kitchen.

The toast was burning. My toast. I rescued it and ate it. I guessed it was because Mom had been poor that she wanted so much. And she had lots of energy. Why shouldn't she use it to build her own business? I admired her for being ambitious, but not for putting the dress shop first. A good mother had to put her kids' needs first.

Avery crawled out from under the table and stood up. "Humans fight too much," he said. "On my starship everybody's going to cooperate." He walked out of the room.

"Sometimes that kid makes more sense than any of us," Dad said. He was rinsing out the empty plastic container in the sink.

"Cinder's not here," Bliss came back to announce. "I looked in every closet. I bet somebody let her out."

"Me maybe, when I came in last night," Dad said. "But don't worry, she'll show up when she's hungry."

"But what if we move first?"

"She's only been gone a few hours," I said. "Maybe she took a vacation, Bliss."

"From me?" Bliss glared at me indignantly.

"I'll keep an eye out for her on my way to Dave's," I said.

"You're not going to stay and help me look?"

"I will if she's not back when I come home, okay?"

"And when you get back, you'd better think about packing," Mom returned in time to say. "Anything not boxed and labeled by the end of the week gets thrown out." She dropped two of the cardboard boxes she'd brought up from the basement onto the kitchen table.

"Maybe Cinder got into a box in the basement. I never looked there," Bliss said hopefully. "Would you go down with me, Daddy?"

"I'm due to give a lesson, honey. I've got to leave."

"Gilda?" Bliss begged.

I knew she was afraid to go to the basement by herself. "All right. All right," I said. I'd let Fettucini wait another five minutes.

"Bring up some boxes when you come back," Mom said.

A mean thought popped into my head. If the wandering Cinder had wandered away for good this time, it would only be Avery who'd have to be persuaded to move to Pam's. Maybe Grandma would spring for a private school for him.

No, I scolded myself. Why should Bliss be the one to suffer? If anyone had to, it should be me. I was the oldest and strongest after all. No, Cinder would come home and we'd move to Mom's apartment next week, and that was the way it would be.

The wind showered me with some last golden leaves as I biked through the deserted streets and I tried to unsnag my spirits from the logjam of bad feelings at home.

Was it true that Mom had wanted to be my friend? I'd always tried hard to please her. Even when I was little, I'd helped with the housework, and when Bliss was born, I'd changed her diapers and fed her and rocked her to sleep. But no matter how much I did, Mom never said, the way I'd heard Stephanie's mother say to her, "I don't know what I'd do without you."

I used to wonder why Mom didn't like me. I thought it was because my size embarrassed her. She spoke softly enough to doll-faced Bliss, and to Avery, who was a boy and "easy," according to Mom, because he lived quietly in his own little world and didn't make any demands on this one. But when she spoke to me, her voice bit with anger.

Maybe living close together in that one-bedroom apartment would help us become friends. In any case, I couldn't let Mom take Bliss and Avery without me. Dad didn't understand. Mom just wasn't home enough hours to take care of them properly.

Dave and his parents were raking leaves in their front yard when I arrived. That was odd because they had an attachment on their tractor to pick up leaves. "What's going on?" I asked.

"Dad's taking pictures for his photography course," Dave said. He laughed as his hefty mother lay down on a pile of leaves and tucked her hands under her cheek as if she were going to sleep. Short, bald, and impish Mr. Curry aimed his camera at her. Then he took pictures of Dave and me chasing each other through the leaves, and one of each of us jumping feet first into a pile. I was laughing so hard by the time Mr. Curry ran out of film that I felt wonderful. Just then Fettucini whinnied from his paddock.

"Poor baby. We kept you waiting so long," I cried, and ran to hug him. Dave had already saddled him for me.

I hoisted myself into the saddle, and Dave came over. "Hey, Gilda, I forgot to tell you. My folks say you're welcome to stay with us as long as you want, but Mom doesn't want to take on younger kids again. I'm sorry."

"Don't be," I said. "It's great they'd take me, and it's nice to know I have an escape hatch if Mom and I get on each other's nerves."

"When're you moving?"

"In a week, Mom says."

He shook his head. "I'm really going to miss you, Gilda."

"Don't make me feel bad," I begged. "We'll see each other weekends, and you'll have the gang at school to keep you company. I'm the one who'll do the missing."

Fettucini pranced down the road, tossing his head in an excess of high spirits. I loved it when he did his wild horse imitation, and I laughed out loud as he kicked up his heels.

It was partly Fettucini's playfulness that had terrified Dave back in fifth grade when his sister had gone off to college and left her horse with him. Dave hadn't wanted to admit to his sister that he was afraid of the pale gray Appaloosa. And when he'd hinted to his father that the horse was too big for him, his father just told him he'd get used to it.

I'd learned all that while we were on the jungle gym

during recess one day. Dave had never spoken to me directly before his sudden outburst. I guess he needed to confide in someone and there I was.

"I'll ride him for you," I had told Dave. "I'd die for a horse. I'll clean out his stall for you, anything you want."

In fifth grade, Mom had only been working part-time. She hadn't invested in the dress shop yet, so my afternoons were free. I'd spent most of them with Dave and Fettucini. By the time Dave overcame his fear, he and I had become best friends. I loved going to his house, because his mother lived the kind of life I wanted someday — except I planned to have more children, at least seven or eight. What impressed me the most, considering how my parents behaved toward each other, was that Mr. and Mrs. Curry never fought, at least not in front of me. "You have the ideal family," I'd told Dave.

"Nothing wrong with yours, is there?" he'd asked.

But he knew. Before the fighting got so bad, Dave used to come to my house sometimes. He'd heard Mom nagging Dad, and Dad complaining to me that Mom got harder to please every year.

Now Fettucini settled down into a brisk walk. We turned onto the path that had been worn through the weeds along the right-of-way under the power line. There I gave him his head, and we cantered between the gawky frameworks that looked like giant Erector-set constructions. Fettucini's gait was so smooth that I seemed to be surfing on air. Trees whizzed by on either side of me and a disturbed crow took off cawing. A rabbit shot across our path, but Fettucini didn't even pretend to be startled.

I let him run until I had to slow him to a walk at the rise before the right-of-way cuts across the bike path, which was where I always turned back. Among the bare-branched trees, only one still kept its deep-wine-colored leaves. Next to it were the reddish torches of the sumac bushes and the white bark of the birch. Even November can be beautiful, I thought, as I looked up at the cluster of birds reeling through the sky.

I rode back slowly, listening to the rhythmic clop of Fettucini's hooves and feeling happier than I'd been in days.

"I love you, Dave," I told him gratefully, after I'd dismounted and taken the saddle off Fettucini.

"Who're you kidding? It's Fettucini you love," Dave said.

"All right, I love you both then. We had the best ride." I kissed the horse's freckled muzzle.

"Mom says to tell you she's got chicken salad for lunch if you want to stay."

"Can't," I said regretfully, sending Fettucini into his paddock. "I promised to get home to look for Cinder, if Bliss hasn't found her already. And Mom wants me to decide what to pack and what to throw out."

"She expects *you* to throw out stuff?" Dave asked. "You, the original pack rat? I bet you've got the first picture you ever drew in kindergarten."

"Yeah, and I still have the first present you ever gave me. Remember what it was?"

He shook his head. "Something goofy?"

"It was a pencil with a fuzzy cat at the eraser end."

He groaned and grinned. Then he said seriously, "I still think you'd be better off going with your father and staying in the same school district."

"*You* just don't want me to move away."

"Right. Who else have I got to talk to?"

I bumped him with my shoulder. "We can talk on the telephone." I wasn't about to feel sorry for Dave. He was the one with the ideal family.

6

Someone was crying. I woke up and saw Bliss sitting up in bed bawling openmouthed. It was three A.M. by the clock on my dresser. I said wearily, "Cinder'll come back. She's disappeared for days before. Don't give up so fast, Blissy."

"But I miss her," Bliss cried. The tears slowed down. She wiped her face with the sleeve of her nightgown and said, "I woke up because my legs felt funny without her there."

"Want to sleep with me?"

"Yes." Bliss promptly bounced out of her bed and into mine. She nestled into me, sighed deeply, and fell right to sleep. During the first five years of her life, she had slept in my bed more often than in her own. It was only after she'd started first grade that I convinced her that she was a big girl now and could sleep alone. The truth is sometimes I miss the warmth of her body next to mine.

What if Cinder was gone for good? What if nobody

answered the posters Bliss and I had tacked up around the neighborhood? Bliss would feel bad for a while, but she'd recover. Then we could get her another animal, something like a guinea pig, a cute furry mop as pettable as a cat and not as likely to disappear. Pam couldn't be allergic to guinea pigs, too. Could Bliss sleep with one, though? I was still considering that question when I dropped off to sleep myself.

Sunday morning Mom drove Bliss around the neighborhood to look for Cinder again. I was packing. I filled the first box with keepsakes — the favorite stuffed toys and dolls I'd saved, my birthday card collection and letters, junk jewelry, articles on self-improvement I'd cut out and mostly not tried, two photograph albums, four unfinished diaries, the sewing box Grandma had sent me that I'd never used. Three full boxes later, I was still finding things in my closet that I had to keep, when Mom stepped into the room. "Gilda, where do you think all that stuff's going?"

I looked up guiltily. "Dave will probably store it for me if nobody else will."

"Good, because no way will all that junk fit into my apartment."

"It's not junk. Just because it's mine and not yours doesn't make it junk." Just to show her, I added, "Anyway, I may still go with Dad to Pam's house."

"You can't scare me with threats like that," Mom said.

"No, because you'd really be just as glad if I didn't jam myself into your apartment."

"So it's my fault, is it? Tell me, do *you* act as if you *want* to be with me?"

"Maybe not, but that's because of how you act."

"We'd get along a lot better if you weren't always trying to show me up, Gilda. I know you think you can do a better job than me, and maybe you're right — but I do my best." Mom gave her eyes a swipe, then turned on her heel and walked out.

I rushed down the hall after her. "Mom!"

"What?"

The tears on her cheeks melted me altogether. "I love you," I said. "No matter what happens to us as a family, I still love you."

Mom accepted my embrace and hugged me back. "Listen," she said, "whoever you go with, it's okay. I won't blame you. I just wish —"

"What?" I asked.

"That we could get along better."

We kissed. It was our most loving moment ever. I returned to my packing feeling happier.

"Avery, what are you *doing?*" I heard Mom ask in his room across the hall.

"Building a starship model," Avery said.

"But I asked you to pack."

"I did," Avery said.

"That little suitcase?"

"And the box. The box has my important stuff."

I was intrigued. As soon as I heard Mom going downstairs, grumbling to herself about her children, I went to see what Avery considered important. When I asked what was in the box, he told me to look. Two books, *Dune* and *Childhood's End*, plus his computer and discs. "No games, no sports stuff?" I asked.

"No, but I'm taking this starship model." His pale face was less dream-clouded than usual. "Want me to explain it to you?"

"Sure." I sprawled on his bed, preparing for one of his endless lectures. On a large sheet of brown wrapping paper taped to the floor, he had drawn an enormous wheel with a hub. Large community rooms where people worked and exercised and met for entertainment were outlined near the hub, he told me. Cubicles for living quarters circled inside the outer edge of the wheel. In between the large rooms and the cubicles were lanes of traffic and overpasses so that people could easily get to any part of the wheel.

I understood that much, but he lost me when he tried to explain more.

"See, you'd be weightless near the hub, so you'd get sick if you hung out there long," he said. "But in the outer rooms — the wheel's spinning, see, so there's gravity in the outer rooms, and it's comfortable there like on earth. And there'll be three-dimensional scenery of like mountains and beaches and deserts projected on the walls that'll seem real. You'll even smell grass and hear stuff like rain and waves, but all the time you're traveling through space."

"Where to?"

"To another star. . . . See, it might take hundreds of years to get there, so it'd be your great-great-grandchild who actually makes it, but that's okay because there'll be plenty to keep you busy on the starship."

"What? You mean people are going to be born and die in this wheel?"

"Well, it's gigantic, Gilda. It's big as a city. And here on earth, plenty of people never leave the city they get born in."

"Yeah, but they know they can."

"Well, maybe there'll be a mind-travel room so you can get away if you need to. . . . Anyway, what's really great is kids don't have to stick to the family they get born into. A kid matches up with an adult who's sort of like him and they stick together. Like say a kid who's good at tennis would spend his time with Dad. And my adult would be a scientist maybe." A smile brightened Avery's face. "And you wouldn't have to go to school. Stuff just gets transmitted directly into your brain like putting in a computer chip."

"Yuck."

"But see, then most of your day you could be working for the greater good. Like you   you'd maybe work in the nursery with the babies if you wanted, or you could be with the horses."

"There'd be horses?" I was glad to hear it. "And do you fall in love and get married in this starship?"

"Yeah, if you want to," Avery said. "Me, I'd skip that part. I'd spend my life in the future-planning group, where they decide how life's going to be when the starship gets somewhere, like, you know, what kind of government and all that."

I looked at Avery's pile of Styrofoam parts and cardboard and Magic Markers and glue. "How are you going to show all that in a model?"

"Well, it's hard. That's why I'm glad I got suspended. This project needs lots of time." He pressed the heels of his hands together in an old gesture of enthusiasm.

I smiled, imagining how surprised his principal would be to find out he'd done Avery a favor. "Av," I said, "tell me why you stole that teacher's code?"

"You won't tell?"

"Promise." I crossed my heart.

"They said they'd stick my head in the toilet and make me eat you know what if I didn't."

"They?"

"You know, those guys in my class that you saw me with? You thought they were my friends, but they hate me, and they'd do it. They're gross. In the starship, guys like that are going to be deprogrammed."

I shuddered. "Sounds pretty drastic, Avery."

"Yeah, well, who needs gross guys anyway?"

"I don't know. Maybe there's a purpose for them."

"Okay, well, if there is — I guess they could be stuck off by themselves somewhere. But then what happens if they grow up and get loose?" He looked alarmed at the idea. "No, I think they should be deprogrammed, Gilda. Don't worry. It won't hurt."

We were talking about an imaginary world, I reminded myself. "Listen, Avery, if Bliss and I were both going to live with Pam, would you come too?"

"Well, see, I want to be with you. You know I do, but going with Mom, I'd get a better chance."

"You mean to be safe or to make a new friend?"

"To be safe," he admitted with some embarrassment.

That figured. Avery had never seemed to much mind being a loner, which meant I only had to deal with his fear. "How about if you were in a different class from the guys who're giving you a hard time?" I asked him.

"No, I need a different school."

What I needed was time to think. "Well, okay," I said. "Talk to you later then." And I left his room.

What could I say? I couldn't promise Avery protection. I could threaten his enemies, but there were no guarantees. Maybe he could somehow get a scholarship to go to the private school where Pam's son went. Avery could use a school where he'd receive special treatment. He was probably some kind of genius.

Could I possibly talk Grandma into paying his tuition? She'd like it that he would be living with his father and sisters instead of with Mom if he could go to a private school. I'd also mention that Avery might be a genius. As soon as I got a chance to call Grandma without the parents overhearing me, I'd plead my case.

More and more it seemed that whether we were going to be living with Dad or Mom depended on Grandma's willingness to help us.

7

Monday morning everybody got ready to leave except Avery. He was cheerfully working away on his starship model. Cinder wasn't home yet, which meant I had to spend half an hour trying to make Bliss stop crying.

"Cinder will come back," I said. "She was gone for a week last time, Bliss. It's way too soon to be scared. I'm sure she's just taking a vacation." I must have sounded more confident than I felt, because Bliss finally dried her tears and got dressed.

I walked into school and there was the turkey on the bulletin board to remind me I only had a week and a half until Thanksgiving. I had better push the parents for decisions, like where we were going to have it. Holidays don't just happen, I'd point out. Turkeys don't materialize stuffed, cooked, and ready to eat. Someone has to prepare them.

The best thing would be for Mom to have the feast at her apartment and invite Dad and Pam and Pauli to come, but Mom wasn't likely to be enthused about that. Maybe Pam would do Thanksgiving at her house and invite Mom. It was going to be awkward for the adults either way, but at least *they* had something to be thankful for — Mom for her freedom, Dad for getting another wife, and Pam for getting Dad. We kids were just losers.

I ducked into the girls' room to use the toilet. Nobody was there until Bebe burst through the door while I was washing my hands.

"Gilda, I'm so glad you're here!" Bebe flung herself into my arms, wet hands and all.

"What's the matter?" I asked.

"He didn't ask me to the eighth-grade dance. He asked Marie."

"Your boyfriend Chris?"

"Yes. He gave me back the leather bracelet I made him. The beast just came to my locker this morning and handed it to me."

"Oh, Bebe. I'm so sorry."

"'I want to break up,' he says. He didn't even say why. I don't know what I did wrong," Bebe wailed.

I rocked her while she sobbed and I told her, "You didn't do anything. I'm sure you didn't do anything, Bebe." I kept rocking and making sympathetic noises until she calmed down. Then I said, "Listen, it's stupid to be miserable, hoping he'll come back to you. You should just pull yourself together and go to the dance with some other guy. That'll show him."

Bebe wiped her eyes and considered the idea. "I'm mad enough to do it."

"Good for you," I said. "That's the spirit."

"But who? Who'd ask me that I'd want to go with?"

"Let's talk about it at lunch. Someone will come up with an idea."

Bebe sighed deeply. "What would I do without you, Gilda? You always make me feel better." She threw me a kiss and hurried out of the bathroom without doing whatever she'd come for, unless it was to have a private cry. There went the bell for the start of homeroom.

What excuse could I give my homeroom teacher today for being late? I could say I felt sick, or, closer to the truth, that I'd overslept. "Don't look at me with those melting brown eyes," my last homeroom teacher used to say.

Did my eyes make Dave melt? He probably didn't notice them one way or the other. One of these days he'd realize how cute he was and get confident enough to ask some pretty girl with narrow hips and slim legs to the school dance. Then Bebe would have to console me. I'd lose Dave fast if I moved to another school, I thought, as I hurried toward my homeroom.

I was lucky. Our homeroom teacher was absent, and the sub didn't even notice when I slipped into my seat five minutes late.

The notice on my desk about a decorations committee meeting for the eighth-grade dance gave me an idea. Dave and I were both on the committee, and the dance was this Friday night, but it might not be too late to get Bebe on the committee too. Pete, Dave's soccer buddy, was on the committee because Dave was, and Pete was quiet and shy but good-looking. If Bebe joined us . . . I wondered if Pete could dance. If not, Dave and I could give him a couple of quick lessons.

I snagged Bebe in the hall on the way to gym and whispered Pete's name to her. "I used to have a crush on him," she whispered back before we broke apart and continued charging on in opposite directions.

Dave was the only male at our lunch table. It didn't seem to bother him until I explained about Bebe needing a date and asked him to ask Pete for her. Then Dave straightened up and glanced around uneasily. "Well, yeah, I could ask him, I guess," Dave said. "But Pete's probably not — I mean, he's pretty shy."

"I know. That's why *you* should be the one to ask him," Bebe said to Dave. "Tell him he doesn't even have to *dance* with me. If he'd just hang out with me so it looks like we're together, that'd be enough."

Dave looked doubtful. "But do you like him?" he asked her.

"Sure. . . . I guess. I mean, he's cute-looking."

"Actually," Steph said, "Pete's a werewolf. You better not let him put his arm around you, Bebe, or you know. Aaaarroo!" She rolled her eyes up.

I laughed, but Bebe pouted. "I wish you wouldn't make fun of me, Stephanie. I'm really upset." Her tears made two delicate chains down her cheeks, which she wiped with the back of her hand.

"Listen," Steph said. "Don't worry. If Pete the werewolf won't take you to the dance, you just borrow your mother's engagement ring and let it be known that a college boy gave it to you. That'll put old what's-his-name in his place."

"My mother'd *never* let me borrow her engagement ring," Bebe said.

"She's just kidding," Jane explained gently.

"You can borrow my mother's," Steph said. "It's fake. It's a big zircon or something."

"An eighth-grade party isn't that big of a deal anyway," Jane said. "Who's going to remember ten years from now who went and who didn't?"

"Me," Bebe said.

Dave looked so cute leaning on his elbow, munching a carrot and listening intently to our chatter. Suddenly I wondered what he'd do if I kissed him. Would he kiss me back if I asked him to? What if he looked disgusted or told me I was crazy? I'd die. Cool it, I told myself. I had enough in my life to feel bad about right now.

The last bell rang, and we dashed for our hall lockers. Dave's was next to mine. I was getting my books and jacket out when he asked me, "So how're things going at home?"

"You must be sick of my family problems, Dave."

"No," he said. "I like hearing about them. I mean, I don't like that you've got trouble. I just — it's interesting." He groaned. "Cut. Let's start again. You're my friend, so I want to hear your problems."

It's a funny thing with me. I like listening to other people's problems and trying to help them, but talking about my own, even to Dave, depresses me. "I'll tell you something good," I said. "Mom was sweet to me this weekend. Maybe she does like me, sort of."

"Well, you only sort of like her, Gilda."

I laughed. "I guess. Anyway, I tried throwing out stuff

78

so I could fit into her apartment, but you were right — I didn't get rid of much. It's like I'm stripping myself of my past. You know what I mean?"

"Why don't you store your past in our barn? It leaks a little, but we could use plastic covers. The folks won't mind."

He was so sweet to me. For the second time that day, I had an urge to kiss him, but I controlled myself and asked instead, "Dave, do you think I have nice eyes?"

"You have beautiful eyes. Come on, Gilda, everyone tells you that."

I batted my lashes at him, making a joke of it. "But I love to hear it."

"Okay. You're a very pretty girl," he said solemnly. Then he whacked me on the back and said, "Come on. This is getting stupid. Let's go."

I smiled all the way home.

When I got there, I saw Dad throwing an armload of clothes into his car. He slammed the door and marched back into the house through the front entrance. No doubt he and Mom had had another fight, which meant she must be home. She'd probably put her car in the garage for a change. I tracked Dad down in the bathroom. He was sweeping the contents of a medicine cabinet shelf into a gym bag, but he dropped his deodorant and his nail clipper. I picked them up for him and asked where he was going.

"You know where," he said. "Anytime you want to join me at Pam's, I'll come get you. Bliss and Avery, too."

"What're you so mad about?"

"Your mother and I had a big fight. So what else is new, right? That's why we're getting divorced. We can't even be civilized to each other anymore."

"What did you fight about?"

"I asked if I could have the reading lamp. It's the only piece of furniture I want. But she claims she paid for it from her earnings. So we fought. After all, we bought the living room and bedroom furniture out of our joint account and — oh, what's the difference? I just got mad. She's getting to be a real — no, listen. It's not right for me to sound off about your mother. . . . I'll talk to you later, honey."

He kissed me on the cheek and left with his plastic bag swinging from his left hand and a hair dryer in his right. It was the hair dryer I used. I never knew it was Dad's. He'd never divvied things up that accurately before. I started bawling, without even knowing I was going to, and ran to my room to cry it out. Bliss was there, lying on her bed.

"What's wrong?" she asked me in alarm.

"Nothing. It's okay, Bliss. Just seeing Dad leaving got to me," I managed to choke out.

"They were fighting," Bliss said calmly.

I wiped my eyes, shuddering as I got control of myself. I didn't want to frighten Bliss, especially when she was already upset about Cinder.

Then Bliss said, "Look. She came back just like you said, Gilda."

I looked and saw a round gray head and pointy ears poking up over the bedspread next to Bliss. I took a deep breath and smiled. "That's great, Blissy. I'm glad for you."

Downstairs I found Mom packing the kitchen things.

"I could really use some help here," she said.

"How come you're home from work?"

"I took a couple of days off to get things organized. But I just can't *do* it all myself." She sounded desperate.

"Okay, I'll help." I was tired from the emotional ups and downs I'd been through, but I knew if I refused to cooperate now, Mom would be mad at me.

I stood on the step stool and handed the dishes down from the top shelves to Mom, who wrapped them in newspaper and packed them in a cardboard box. While I worked, I thought about our options. Going to Pam's was out now that Cinder was back, which meant there was no point in asking Grandma about a private school for Avery. Cinder's return sure simplified things. Mom's apartment was our only choice.

Dave called that evening to tell me to watch a television special on wild horses. "Dave, would your mother drive you across town to visit me sometimes, do you think?"

Silence . . . "You decided?"

"It's been decided. Cinder came back, and my father moved out today."

"Yeah? Well, you knew he was going to."

"But seeing him do it —" My voice cracked. "I mean, we were a family for my whole life and now we're not anymore."

"Yeah," Dave said. "Well, you can ride your bike over to his girlfriend's house and see him whenever you want, can't you?"

"I'd rather go live with Dad than with Mom. A lot rather."

"So why don't you?"

"Because Mom won't be around when Bliss and Avery need her. They'll get sick and she'll be too busy to notice, and they'll live on junk food."

"Come on, Gilda. Your mother's not that bad."

"Isn't she? Oh, well," I said bitterly, "at least she'll dress them in the latest styles because *that* she considers important. She thinks *I'm* a dud because I like to wear comfortable clothes. Well, I can't *wear* the latest styles. They never look good on me." I sounded whiny. I knew it, but I couldn't help myself.

I sniveled a little more and admitted, "Anyway, I need Avery and Bliss with me."

"Oh. Then you're not just going for their sake, huh?" He had made his point. I sucked in my breath and didn't answer. He waited a minute and then said, "Well, what are we going to tell Fettucini?"

"I don't know." I wished he hadn't pointed out that I wasn't as unselfish as I pretended to be.

"Listen," Dave said. "You can still ride him weekends. It's not like you're moving to Australia."

"So you think I should accept how it is and make the best of a bad deal, right?"

"That's the advice you'd give me."

It was a lot easier to give that kind of advice than to take it. "It's a really long bike ride, Dave," I complained. "I don't even know *how* long it is from that apartment to your house. . . . I haven't even *seen* the apartment yet."

"Yeah, well, in a few years I'll get my learner's permit, and meanwhile my mom won't mind driving me over, or picking you up and bringing you here. . . . Hey, maybe you can come for a sleepover."

I had to laugh. "And have the whole school talking about us?"

"Anyway, I made you laugh," he said.

"You did. Thanks."

"So when are you moving?"

"Saturday Mom's having a garage sale, and the guys she hired to move us are supposed to come in the middle of it unless she can talk them into coming Friday. It's going to be a mess."

"And Friday night's the dance," Dave reminded me. "Should be an interesting weekend."

Interesting wasn't the word for it — depressing maybe, confusing, upsetting. I dreaded the coming weekend, even if the dance was part of it. And the Thursday following it was Thanksgiving, and I still hadn't settled anything about that.

8

Mom forbade me to use the word "Thanksgiving" in her presence until after the move to her apartment. "My head's bursting with too many details already, Gilda. Don't bug me about Thanksgiving for cripes sake."

I tried Dad, who looked at me blankly and said he guessed he'd be with Pam and I was welcome to join them. When I asked him about Bliss and Avery, he walked out on me. Then he wouldn't talk about Thanksgiving either. It was maddening. *They* were maddening, but I gritted my teeth and vowed to be patient. There was bound to be a turkey left in some store somewhere, even if we waited until the day before the holiday to buy it — which seemed to be what was going to happen.

Since Cinder's return, Bliss had barely let her kitten's feet touch the ground. I saw Cinder even clinging to Bliss's sweater by one paw like an acrobat while busily washing herself with her elastic pink tongue.

Now that she had Cinder back, Bliss seemed calm about the move. "Did you tell anybody in school that you're leaving?" I asked her.

"The teacher told them. They don't care, Gilda. Just one boy. He likes me."

"Oh? So you have a boyfriend. Good for you, Bliss. Is he nice?"

"Uh-uh." Bliss shook her head. "He eats liverwurst sandwiches and smells yucky."

I guessed Bliss wasn't going to miss *him* much.

The principal had given in and allowed Avery to return to school Tuesday without having ratted on anyone. "Did those kids give you any grief?" I asked Avery when he got home Tuesday afternoon.

"No. They just said I was lucky I didn't tell on them."

"So you still want to change schools?"

"Yeah."

That left no one but me to be miserable about the move. When Mom asked me to go with her to see the new apartment, I refused. "I don't want to look at it until I have to," I said.

"Suit yourself," she told me. I knew I was being stubborn, but I didn't care.

Friday, Bliss and Avery stayed home from school to wait with Mom for the moving truck, which she had managed to reschedule. They were going to follow the truck to the new apartment in Mom's car. Since the dance was that evening, I said I'd take my dress and shoes with me to school and go from there to Dave's. His mother was driving us to the party. What's more, if

Mom didn't want to pick me up after the party, I could stay overnight at Dave's.

Mom thought that was a great idea. "You can meet me here Saturday," she said. "I have to come back anyway to help that woman I hired to do the garage sale."

"You mean I have to *watch* someone buy my bedroom set? Mom!"

"Tell you what," she said with sudden sympathy. "Get someone to store your furniture for you, and I'll have the moving truck deliver it there. Whatever we'd get for those pieces won't be worth the effort you put into stripping and painting them."

"Thanks!" I said, and hugged her gratefully. I considered Dave's barn, but decided the furniture would be safer in one of Pam's empty rooms. Making Dad change his mind about not using her place as a storage facility shouldn't be hard. He knew how much that furniture meant to me. "I'll ask Pam if I can stow stuff in one of her third-floor bedrooms," I said.

"Three floors? What's she need with a house that big?" Mom asked.

"She inherited it."

"I see. So your father's returning to his own kind."

"Mom, Dad picked a woman who's just like you," I said.

"Like me? Fat chance. Your father met her at Union College before he dropped out. Her parents paid for her to go there. I attended the evening session of the community college, which I paid for myself." Mom got herself a glass of water. "She probably thinks saving money is buying an expensive dress on sale. Me, I save by doing without. No way is that woman like me, Gilda."

"That's why you're working so hard to make this dress shop a success, because you were poor," I said with sympathy.

"Who said I was poor? I never went hungry. I always had a place to sleep. I just didn't have much. And that's no shame," Mom said.

"Of course it isn't." Mom's prickliness was frustrating. "Are you sorry you said you wanted all three of us?" I asked. "It's going to crowd you."

"What are you looking for, Gilda, an excuse to go stay with your father in his girlfriend's big house? Go, if you want. I'm not going to hold you back."

"Mom, really! What I want is to be with both you and Dad. I want our family to stay whole more than anything in the world."

"Then I guess you're going to be disappointed. Sorry, kid," Mom said.

End of conversation.

Not only did Pam cheerfully agree to take the furniture when I called to ask her, but she also said, "Just have the movers pack it in any empty room on the third floor. And you can consider the room yours, Gilda."

I must have thanked her six different times. The luxury of my own space whenever I wanted it was an unexpected gift, and I was grateful.

Friday afternoon, instead of biking directly to Dave's with my party dress neatly folded in a box in my backpack, I detoured past my house for one last look. I expected the place to seem deserted with most of the furniture gone, but it looked the same from the outside. A red plastic cardinal I'd made at summer camp years ago still hung in the glass pane of the front door. I decided to keep it as a memento of the old homestead.

My key worked, but when I walked inside, it startled me to see Avery sitting at the kitchen table. "What are you doing here still?" I asked.

"The moving truck broke down, so they're not coming until tomorrow. Mom's mad because now the movers'll get mixed up with the garage sale."

"And where's Mom?"

"She took a carload of stuff to her apartment. Bliss went, too, to show Cinder where she's going to live."

Avery was cutting out magazine pictures of people. "For your starship?" I asked, sitting down across from him.

"Yeah. They'll give the idea of how the rooms can be used. And you know what, Gilda? I'm going to have a port where flyers can get out and sail around in space with big wings like kites."

"That's nice." I was busy estimating how many meals I'd eaten in this kitchen, thousands probably. But there wouldn't be any more.

"See the energy all comes from one direction — you know — from the sun," Avery continued enthusiastically, "but you can tack across it just like a sailboat does with the wind on earth. So you can sail out from the starship and back in. See?"

"Amazing," I said, and smoothed his hair back from his eyes. Someday, no doubt, I'd sit in an audience listening to my brother, the scientist, lecturing. I probably wouldn't understand him any better than I did now, but that wouldn't stop me from being proud of him.

I roamed through the house in a kind of trance, as if I had already moved away and this wasn't my home anymore. But it had been. Here both Avery and Bliss fell down the stairs. Mom said I did, too, but I don't remember. In my room, a big pile of boxes waited for the movers. I might have to leave some stuff *in* the boxes if Mom's apartment was really tiny.

Don't whine, I told myself. It's people, not places, that matter. I stuck out my chin and started whistling. Dave had taught me how last summer, but I was so bad that mostly we'd had fun laughing at my attempts.

Avery appeared in my doorway. "I've got a problem, Gilda."

"What?" I went on ready alert instantly. It didn't surprise me that he wasn't taking this move as easily as he'd pretended he was. "Tell me."

"Well, the clothes are wrong. People on the starship wouldn't be wearing clothes like us," he said.

False alarm. I should have known my brother better. It would take a lot more than a move to bring him in from outer space. "They might," I told him. "After all, your spaceship's climate controlled inside, isn't it?"

"Starship. Yeah, I guess, but it's supposed to be like twenty years from now."

"Twenty years from now what we're wearing will be back in style," I said.

"Oh, yeah? Hey, neat. Thanks, Gilda."

I left him happy in his future world. Probably Bliss was happy, too, in the apartment with Mom. And me? I got on my bike and headed for Dave's. The pack on my back was the least of the things weighing me down.

Dave and I were standing side by side in his flagstone entry hall. "Don't move," his father said. A minute later he came back with his camera. "This is an historic occasion," he said. "Dave dressed up for his first date. Hold hands or something, kids."

"It's not a date," Dave said, and backed away from me hastily. "We're only going because we're on the committee."

"But it's close to being a date," his mother said. "And you both look really nice."

"Thanks, Mrs. Curry," I said. Dave looked like a handsome junior business executive in his suit. As for me, I was wearing a navy blue shirtwaist that made me look slimmer, but also a lot older. Dave had squinted at me oddly when I walked downstairs dressed for the dance, and he hadn't complimented me. I wished I'd picked something bright or cute instead of a dress that looked like a blue uniform, but it was too late now.

The decorating committee hadn't managed to disguise the school cafeteria much with the sheaves of corn, fake fruit, and gold foil garlands. Dave's friend Pete hurried over when he saw us. "My tie's too tight," he said. "I'm choking."

"So loosen it," Dave said.

"I don't know how. Pop tied it."

"Oh, let me!" Bebe said. She had just come up behind us. Pete ducked and ran. We caught up with him at the railing in front of the food counter just as the three-piece band began to play.

Bebe grabbed Pete's arm to convince him he was trapped. Then, while he blushed and fidgeted, she fussed with his tie. "There now. That's fixed." She took hold of his arm again. "So are we going to dance?"

"Now?" Pete squeaked. The space that had been left for a dance floor was so empty it was frightening.

"Pete, come on out on the floor with me," Bebe begged. "You can just stand there and kind of rock in time to the music. You can even close your eyes if you want."

Obviously Bebe hadn't meant it when she said all Pete had to do was show up and stand near her. She tugged at him, and he followed her onto the dance floor like a dog on a leash. When poor Pete actually did close his eyes, Dave and I both started laughing.

"Let's go, Gilda." Dave punched my arm and led the way. The sister who'd left him Fettucini had also taught him to dance. In fact, she'd taught him so well that kids quickly made a circle around us to watch. I felt self-conscious being on display, but I know I'm graceful on a dance floor even though I'm big, so I let go and danced.

"It was wonderful," I enthused to Dave later, as we walked out the side door to the parking lot where his father was to pick us up. "And you're a wonderful dancer. I had such a —"

"Wonderful time," Dave mocked me gently. "Yeah, me too. . . . Hey, hold still a minute." He grabbed my arm, stopping me in a dark area where we were shielded from the parking lot by a screen of evergreens.

"What's wrong?" I looked around in alarm.

That was when he kissed me. Bing bang, just like that. "There," he said with satisfaction. "I did it."

"Congratulations," I said, and grabbed him to kiss him back. Then I ran giddily to the lineup of parental cars, where Mr. Curry was waiting.

Going home, I sat quietly while Dave told his father about the dance. I was so happy. Hulk that I was, Dave Curry had kissed me of his own free will. For sure that meant that some guy someday would want to marry me, and unlike my parents, I'd stay married. Seven children would be nice, eight maybe, and a house in the country with a vegetable garden and a big kitchen like Mrs. Curry had.

Saturday morning when I returned to the old house for the garage sale, Mom greeted me with a new crisis. "Gilda, Bliss's run away."

"How come?"

"That cat. We bumped into the building manager when we were unloading the car at my apartment yesterday, and he saw Cinder and told us absolutely *no* pets are allowed. It's in the lease. I never noticed. I was just so glad to get the place."

"You mean, Bliss has been gone since yesterday?"

"No. But she wasn't here when I got up this morning."

"Did you check all her friends' houses?"

"I've called everyone, including your father. He'll be over in a few minutes. Where would she go, Gilda?" Mom looked terrified.

I thought fast. "Did you ask Avery if Bliss said anything to him?"

"He doesn't know anything. Anyway I can't get him to stop cutting and pasting. And the moving men are due and the garage sale's starting. Oh, cripes! Why does everything I do turn out to be such a hassle? Find Bliss for me, please."

"I'll try."

The moving truck pulled up, and a man got out with papers in his hand. Mom dashed over to him. Two women were tagging items in the garage — gardening tools, and shelves of books, and lamps and toys. The telephone rang. "Gilda! Get that, will you?" Mom called.

I squeezed into the house, past an elderly couple who had apparently come early to shop the garage sale, which wasn't supposed to start until ten.

Grandma was on the phone.

"I wanted to know how you children are making out," she said. The sympathy in her voice was all it took to break me down.

"It's bad, Grandma. Bliss ran away because Mom can't have cats in her apartment, and Dad can't take Cinder because his — because Pam's allergic."

"The poor child!" Grandma said. "Well, when you find her, you tell her she can bring her cat and come stay with me. Tell her I'll even rent a piano for her."

"In New York? But where would she go to school?"

"I'll send her to a good private school for girls. I'm on the board, and they owe me a favor. I'd be happy to send her."

"What about Avery and me?"

Grandma hesitated. Then she said, "You mean all of you want to come down here? I don't know, Gilda. *Three* children at my age would be more responsibility than I — and Avery's so addle-brained. And you're a teenager. Besides, my apartment would burst at the seams."

"I guess so," I said. Being rejected hurt, but Grandma was making sense, except the part about my being a teenager — as if that automatically made me a trouble-maker. Not that I wanted to live in New York City anyway. I'd never see Dave or my friends or Fettucini then. Or my parents. "I'll tell Bliss what you said when I find her," I said, and hung up.

I hoped Bliss wasn't going to be tempted by the piano and decide to go to Grandma's. On the other hand, if Bliss didn't stay with Mom, then why should I? Avery was old enough to be alone after school. I might as well go to Pam's with Dad. But that would put all three of us in different places. And that would be rotten.

I found Bliss at her music teacher's house.

"Bliss asked if I'd mind if she just sat in my den and watched television while the moving men were at her house," the music teacher explained.

Bliss was in the teacher's den, sprawled in front of the television set with Cinder coiled in her lap and a can of soda in her hand. She even had a bag of chips conveniently open beside her. "Hi, Gilda," Bliss said.

"How long were you going to hang out here?"

"Until everybody goes. Then I'm going to sneak back in the house and live there with Cinder all by myself."

"And who's going to feed you?"

"Somebody will." She chomped on a chip.

"Oh, sure." I plunked down on the couch and extended my finger. Cinder licked it delicately before turning her head back against Bliss's leg. "Grandma says she'll take you and Cinder and throw in a piano if you want to move to New York."

"She will?" Bliss's face brightened.

"You want to live in New York while the rest of us are way up here in Niskayuna?"

"You come too, Gilda."

"Grandma doesn't want me. Just you."

"Well . . ." Bliss considered. "Where else can Cinder and me go?"

I shook my head in despair. "I don't know. . . . Bliss, don't I matter more to you than your cat?"

"But Cinder needs me," Bliss said. "You don't need me, Gilda. You can take care of yourself."

How could I argue with logic like that? "It looks as if I may have to," I said. Then I called Mom to tell her Bliss was found.

9

I expected Mom to have a fit when Bliss told her at breakfast that she wanted to go stay with Grandma in New York. To my surprise, Mom just gave Bliss a hawk-eyed stare and asked, "What'd she promise you to bring that about?"

Bliss looked at me for help. I said, "Grandma says Cinder's welcome, too, and she'll get Bliss a piano."

Mom snorted and told Bliss, "Fine. If you think you'll be happy living with your grandma on Fifth Avenue, go right ahead and try it."

So then why did Mom get furious when I told her I thought I might as well follow my furniture to Pam's? We were standing in the empty living room, watching the movers cart out the couch, but Mom didn't care who heard her. She yelled, "Well, that takes the cake! Don't I mean anything to you at all, Gilda?"

"Mom, it's not you," I protested. "But as long as Bliss doesn't need me, why should I give up my life here? You and Avery can manage fine without me, and as soon as you get a place that'll take Cinder, Bliss and I will move back in with you."

"Don't give me that Avery and me business," Mom said. "You're only thinking of yourself."

"So? Why shouldn't I? *You* put yourself first, don't you?"

"Me?" Mom cried. "You mean it's all my fault. What about your father? *He's* the one who's got a girlfriend."

"But he only got the girlfriend after you decided to get divorced," I said. "Anyway, Dad has Pam, and you've got your dress shop and that support group you go to every week. You've both got what you want. We're the only ones who didn't get anything, Avery and Bliss and me."

I was sorry the minute I let the words out of my mouth. Mom turned beet red. "You think being a mother's easy?" she screamed. "Someday you're going to find out it's not."

I was biting my lip to keep from yelling back, when Dad sauntered into the living room. "What's this — World War Three?" he asked.

"What are you doing here?" Mom wanted to know.

"I came over to see if I could help."

"Good. I'm glad somebody's offering." Mom's face was wet with tears.

Seeing her cry made me feel so bad that I wanted to hug her and say I loved her and was sorry. I tried, but she shook me off. "I'll tell the movers to drop your boxes off with your furniture, Gilda," she said. "You'd better call that woman and make sure you're welcome."

"It's okay with Pam if I move into her house, isn't it, Dad?" I asked.

"Sure, she'd be glad to have you," Dad said.

Mom turned her back on me. I felt like a traitor, but I knew from past experience that it would be best to let her cool down before trying to apologize again.

"I'd better find Avery and let him know what's up," I said.

Avery was in his bedroom staring out the window.

"What're you doing, Av?"

"I'm just thinking. If I act cool like the other kids, they won't think I'm weird in the new school. Right, Gilda?"

"It's worth a try — if you care what they think," I said.

"I sort of care, a little," Avery said.

He never had before. I guessed he was growing up, and that was good, even though it made me sad somehow. I explained that now he was going to be the only one living with Mom and why. "You don't mind, do you?" I asked.

He hunched up his shoulders. "I don't know. Just me?"

"Just you and Mom. If you get lonely, you can join me at Pam's."

"I won't get lonely . . . I don't think. I'm not a baby." He smiled at me, but his cheek was twitching and one side of his face was only half a smile high. "Will you come over and see my model when it's finished?"

"You bet."

"I'll call you," he said. "I can call you, can't I, Gilda?"

"Sure, every night if you want. And I can ride my bike over to see you whenever you need me."

He nodded, but he looked anxious.

By midafternoon, a "Sold" banner had been pasted across the "For Sale" sign on the front lawn. At the curb, boxes of unwanted things waited in uneven stacks to be carted off to the dump. What hadn't sold at the garage sale but was too good to throw away would be taken to the Salvation Army bins and left there.

I helped Mom lift a box of books into the trunk of her car. Dad tied a lamp table onto a rack he'd improvised on top of the car. Mom sagged against the door in exhaustion. "Want me to drive the other stuff over to the Salvation Army place?" Dad asked.

"That's okay," Mom said. "I can handle it."

"I don't mind," he said.

She shrugged. "If you want to do something I'd really appreciate, drive Bliss down to your mother's for me."

"You mean today?"

My heart kicked in my chest. "Not today," I said.

"When then?" Mom demanded. "She's got to go to school somewhere on Monday. Why should she start a new school near me when she'll be going to one in New York?"

"We could drive her down together tomorrow," Dad said.

"Not me," Mom said. "*I'm* not going with you."

"Mother'll chew me out for letting our marriage fall apart," Dad said.

"So? You're a big boy, Skip. You don't have to be afraid of what your mama says. Anyway, she's probably glad you're getting rid of me."

"You're wrong, Tina," Dad said. "She's big on family togetherness. She'll say I should have hung on to you."

"Fat chance. She never liked me. She blames me that we got married so young. She thinks I got pregnant to trap you."

"With me?" I asked, but they were so wound up in each other they didn't even hear.

"She blamed us both for that," Dad said.

"Yes, your mother's the blame-laying expert."

Dad ignored that last crack and turned to me. "Gilda, you'll come help me with Grandma, won't you?" He gave me a one-armed hug.

"Sure," I agreed. "I'd like to go. I haven't seen Grandma since she visited us last summer."

Mom glared at me.

"Avery can come too," Dad said. "Mother always complains we never bring the grandchildren to see her. Let's get started if we're going, Gilda."

"Now?" I couldn't believe it. Now — it was happening now!

"Then I might as well get over to my apartment and start unpacking by myself," Mom said. "I'm exhausted already."

"Well," Dad said, "this whole move *was* your idea, Tina."

"You agreed to it fast enough. It gave you an excuse to move in with your girlfriend."

"She's *not* my girlfriend. Pam's my future wife."

"I hope you warned her the only place you hustle is on a tennis court. Or does she expect you to be handy at fixing that big old house of hers?"

"Hey, you guys!" I begged, but they were already in the thick of battle.

". . . And you can tell your mother she's not doing me any favor sending Bliss to a private school, trying to turn her into a little snob."

"You want to fight with Mother, call her up and do it yourself," Dad said.

"It's only fair, I guess," Mom replied, her voice rising. "She failed with you, so now she gets to try again with Bliss."

"Right. So I'm a failure to my mother and a failure to my wife." Dad opened his mouth, clamped it shut, and said, "Okay, what's the difference? Gilda, get the kids and let's get started. It's a three-hour drive."

"Bliss's things are at my apartment," Mom said. "You'll have to pick them up."

"No problem; it's on the way to the Thruway." Dad turned to me and urged, "Come on, honey. We can eat supper in the city."

I walked across the bare living room and into the kitchen, feeling as if I were inside a nightmare where things looked familiar but weren't quite normal. The family structure that I'd hung my whole life on was collapsing as suddenly as if an earthquake had hit us. I was separating from my mother, my house, my sister and brother. What had seemed so comfortingly solid was fragile as glass. I felt sick to my stomach.

Out in the backyard I found Bliss sitting on a stump,

listening to Avery, while Cinder swatted a pinecone around. "Gilda," Bliss called to me, "you know Avery's got a zoo room on the starship? And people can keep cats, but the cats can't have kittens. Except one cat can. I hope it's Cinder."

"Cinder's not going to be on the starship," Avery said. "She'll be dead by the time it gets built up there in space."

"She will not!"

"Sure she will. Cats only live about twenty years. You'll be grown up and maybe have kids of your own before this ship gets built, Bliss."

"Listen, Avery," I said, interrupting the discussion. "Dad and I are driving Bliss down to Grandma's, and we want you to come, too."

"Gilda," Bliss put in, "stay with me at Grandma's, okay? Because I'll be lonely without you."

"I'll be lonely without her, too," Avery said. "I won't have anyone to talk to."

"You'll have Mom," Bliss said.

"But Mom doesn't hear what I tell her."

"Well, I can't be everyplace," I said, but I was pleased that they needed me, so pleased I could say cheerfully, "Listen, this'll just be a temporary separation. We'll be together for Thanksgiving, and then we can figure a way to get back together permanently. Okay?"

"When's Thanksgiving?" Bliss asked.

"Next Thursday," I said.

Tears filmed Bliss's eyes.

"You can still change your mind," I said. "If you don't want to go to Grandma's, you don't have to."

"But what about Cinder?" Bliss wailed. "Nobody else will take her and me both."

"Maybe Mom and Dad will change their minds, and not get divorced," Avery, the dreamer, said.

"Let's tell them if they don't love each other again, we'll run away," Bliss suggested.

"We don't have anyplace to run to," I pointed out.

"If Avery's starship was built, we could go there," Bliss said.

Avery shook his head. "Gilda wouldn't want to," he said. "She likes the Earth."

"Yeah, I do," I said. "How'd you know that, Av?" It touched me that my spacey brother, who was barely aware of the people around him, should know that about me. "I like people and horses and the way the wind blows leaves and clouds around. I wouldn't want to live out in space."

"Anyway," Bliss said, as much to herself as to us, "I'll take my music sheets, and I'll practice everyday on Grandma's piano, and Cinder can sleep in my bed."

"And I'll work on my starship," Avery said.

And I would continue seeing Dave and riding Fettucini, I thought. I might even get more of Dad's attention than I'd had in years, being the only one of his children living with him. "It won't be so bad," I said. "And we'll definitely be together on Thanksgiving."

"Where?" Bliss asked.

"I don't know yet," I said. "But somewhere." And I hustled them off to Dad's car and the drive down to New York.

10

We must have looked pretty strange as we walked single file for five blocks from the parking space Dad had found to Grandma's apartment, because people turned to stare at us. Each of us was toting a box of Bliss's belongings. Cinder was crying in her plastic pet carrier, and Bliss kept saying, "It's okay, Cinder. Don't be scared." The narrow streets between the tall blocky buildings seemed dingy to me. If Grandma had so much money, why had she lived here for forty years, including the whole time Dad was growing up? Why hadn't she moved to a greener, cleaner place?

Then the new doorman wouldn't let us in. He eyed us suspiciously as if we were homeless people trying to invade his building, but he did call Grandma on the intercom to ask about us. She must have given him the okay, because he finally opened the door and directed us to the elevator. "It's on the fifth floor and to the left."

"We know," Dad said shortly. I could tell he didn't

like the doorman's attitude either. Well, if we'd visited Grandma more often, the doorman might have recognized us. We carried our boxes through the carpeted lobby, past the carved walnut chairs and into the elevator.

Grandma was waiting at her door with a faint smile and a cool cheek for us to kiss. She smelled lovely. The first thing I noticed in her foyer was the piano. Grandma must have ordered it the instant she heard Bliss was coming. Bliss squealed with delight over the piano as I looked around the dim, quiet apartment. Nothing else had changed since my last visit a few years ago. Off the big foyer was a closet-sized kitchen, a bathroom, and a small bedroom. Grandma's big, light-filled bedroom was at the front, next to the long, narrow living room. Except for the original oil paintings in heavy gilt frames on the walls, the room looked plain. Grandma never bought anything new, never did anything different, and never traveled either. Being rich was wasted on her.

She looked older to me, stiff and fragile in a gray wool dress that matched her hair, but her voice had its familiar authority as she told us to stow the boxes in the small bedroom. That was to be Bliss's. As soon as she got into the room, Bliss unlatched the door to the pet carrier. Cinder leaped out and promptly hid under the bed.

"Just be sure you clean the kitty-litter pan every day, Bliss," Grandma said. Then she turned to Dad and announced, "With such short notice, I couldn't cook dinner for you, so I'm taking you all out to eat tonight. If we go now, you should be done in time to get home before midnight." Her smile dropped off, and she added hastily, "Unless of course you'd like to spend the night. You're welcome, but you'd have to sleep on the couch, Skip, and I don't know how comfortable —"

"That's okay, Mother. We'd planned to go back tonight," he said.

Grandma nodded with relief. "Tomorrow I've got tickets to a concert at Carnegie Hall. Fortunately, my friend can't go, so Bliss can be my companion instead."

"I've never been to a real concert," Bliss said.

"Well, I'll see to it you're exposed to plenty of them while you're here," Grandma promised.

It wasn't until we were in the restaurant waiting for dinner to be served that Grandma asked how things were going in Niskayuna. Dad told her the house was sold and she sighed. She sighed again when he described where Avery and I were going to live. "And how do you feel about all of this?" Grandma turned to me to ask.

"I hate it."

"Of course," Grandma said. She glanced at Avery, who was concentrating on eating his pasta with pesto sauce. She didn't ask him how *he* felt. Instead, she said to Dad, "It's the children who suffer most."

Dad's boyish face flushed, but Grandma didn't push the attack, and Dad relaxed again.

After seeming perfectly happy and enjoying a big hunk of chocolate mousse cake for dessert at the restaurant, Bliss got back to the apartment and burst into tears when it was time to say good-bye. She clung to me as if she hadn't understood we were going to be separated and was just now realizing it.

"You'd better go," Grandma said to Dad. "Long good-byes just make things worse." She gave Avery a quick kiss on the cheek and asked him if he knew her telephone number in case he needed her for something. He shook his head. Grandma then told him the number and made him write it down. "Don't lose that now," she said. "You keep your eyes open, Avery, and pay attention to what's going on around you, hear?"

"Yes, Grandma," Avery said.

She let Dad and me kiss her good-bye, and then rushed us out of her apartment as if she wanted to get rid of us.

"Don't worry about Bliss, Gilda," Dad told me in the elevator. "Your grandmother'll settle her down in no time."

"I know," I said, thinking of the piano and the concerts and Cinder's presence. "But what about me?"

"Listen," Dad said, "if you miss baby-sitting, you can always do it for pay."

"It's my sister I'm going to miss, not the sitting," I said.

Suddenly he stopped being flip and broke down. "I know, honey. I know," he said. "This whole thing is lousy. I hate it that you kids can't even stay together. I messed up bad. But your Mom and I just can't live with each other anymore. We can't, Gilda, and it's likely we'll all be better off once we get through this. Don't you think? . . . Anyway, it's possible, isn't it?"

I'd made my mother cry, and now Dad was crying. When the elevator stopped, he took out a handkerchief and began blowing his nose to get control of himself.

"You still got me, Gilda," Avery said.

"You'll be at Mom's."

"Well, but you can ride your bike over anytime you need me," Avery said.

"Thanks, Av." I squeezed his hand. He even squeezed back.

In the lobby by the carved chairs we stood and hugged each other, Dad and Avery and I. Still, walking to the car in the shadowy light of the streetlamps, three now where we had been four, I leaked a few tears. And on the drive home, I stared out at the red, green, and white gemstone lights of the city, thinking how sad it was that the city should be most beautiful at night, that it needed the lights to disguise how worn and gray ·it was.

Dad switched on the radio to a rock-and-roll station and turned up the volume so that the music beat down on us as we drove along the Thruway. I opened my mouth to complain that it was so loud we couldn't talk, but then I shut my mouth. What was there to say? It was sensible that Bliss stay with Grandma, and Avery with Mom, and me with Dad. Being together was just not practical anymore, no matter how much I wanted it.

By the time we'd dropped Avery off at Mom's and

driven to Pam's, it was late and the house was dark. I crept upstairs to the third-floor bedroom where Dad said my furniture had been placed. It was arranged the way it had been at home, but in Pam's house I had a view of treetops through the window. Streetlamps in halos of light shone up at me through bare tree branches. The day had been so hectic, I was sure I'd fall asleep easily; but I didn't. I was feeling too bad.

The next morning was Sunday. Pam was making pancakes in the kitchen, already dressed in jeans and a freshly ironed cotton shirt. She gave me a short smile and warned, "This is the only day of the week I do breakfast. The other six, you're on your own. Anything special you need for breakfasts and lunches?"

"I eat everything," I said. "Usually cereal for breakfast. And I buy lunch in school."

"Good," she said. "But just to be sure we don't trip over each other's hangups, I wrote down the house rules for you. Whatever you think I should know, you can tell me or write me a note about it. And if I don't like something you're doing, you can be sure you'll find a note from me on the refrigerator. Communicating's an effort, but it avoids misunderstandings."

"Sure," I said. But I asked curiously, "What are the house rules?"

My answer was a typed sheet of paper. Reading it, I learned that Pam set limits on everything:

Telephone calls restricted to three minutes with anything longer requiring an explanation. Shower time five minutes, or for a bath — don't fill the bathtub more than 2/3 full. Clean the bathroom after you use it. You clean your own room. If it isn't properly cleaned, you pay a fine which goes toward extra hours pay for the cleaning person to do it for you. Permission must be granted to have friends visit, and visits made to friends' houses should be noted on the chalkboard by the telephone along with a telephone number and name where you can be reached. No music after ten P.M. No loud music at any time. Adults get first choice of what television program to watch. In case of kids' conflict, you take your turn at first choice. One can of soda per day or provide your own.

The last lines were, "In a happy home, people are courteous and considerate of each other at all times. Let's make ours a happy home."

I finished reading and gulped. Pam didn't know me if she thought I needed a set of rules to get along in a new place.

"Any problem with anything on that?" Pam asked.

"What if I forget something?" I said to test her.

"You'll get used to doing it my way," she said briskly. "It eliminates a lot of hassles." She told me where the dishes and silverware were and asked how many pancakes I wanted.

"Three?" I said, but I could see there wasn't much batter left in the bowl, so I added, "Or two is enough."

Pam gave me three and joined me at the table with a cup of coffee. I felt sloppy sitting across from her in my robe. Her eyes were as bright and sharp as her man-tailored shirt, and her short, well-shaped nails were perfectly polished. No sleepy morning person, this was one efficient lady. I wondered what my easygoing father was doing with a powerhouse like Pam.

"Your father's giving Pauli a tennis lesson this morning," Pam said. "Then we thought we'd take a drive into the Adirondacks and do a little hiking. Want to come?"

"Sure, if you can wait until I ride Fettucini — that's my friend Dave's horse. I usually ride him for an hour or so first thing when I get up on Sundays, and then sometimes I eat Sunday dinner at Dave's."

"Doesn't sound as if you have time for both the hike and the ride. We'll be leaving in less than an hour."

"Maybe I could go with you next time then," I said. "Dave kind of expects me. I guess I'll spend the day with him."

"Fine. Just leave his number on the board and the time we can expect you home. We'll probably be back late."

Again I got a measured amount of smile. Pam was so crisp I imagined that she'd crunch if you bit into her, like celery, like a radish. Did she have any soft spots? Or weren't soft and gentle the kind of qualities Dad admired in a woman? It made me uneasy to find

111

I didn't understand my own father all that well. I thought I knew him, but I'd never have picked Pam as someone he'd fall for. As for me, I could live with her rules because they seemed fair enough, but they didn't exactly make me feel at home in her house.

I decided to call Avery later from Dave's house to check on how he was doing, but when I got to Dave's, I realized I'd left Mom's new telephone number on the dresser. Maybe if I got back to Pam's before the hiking group did, I could call Avery then.

The long ride on Fettucini under the power lines was so soothing that I was relaxed by the time I joined Dave on his back porch. He looked up from the funny papers and asked, "So how goes it?"

"Bad," I said. "Yesterday I had a mother and a father and a brother and sister living with me, and today the only one left is Dad. I don't know. I always imagined families were part of you, like your arms and legs, not something stuck on with Velcro that you could pull apart."

"Ah, come on, Gilda. You haven't lost your family."

"We're not together anymore."

"That's just temporary."

"So they say. Anyway, I've got to make Dad understand about Thanksgiving. If we don't share holidays at least, we won't even *be* a family anymore."

"Yeah, my mom's big on sharing, too," Dave said. "Thursday this place will be a madhouse. My sisters are coming home from college with their boyfriends and roommates, and my married brother's bringing his mother-in-law, and my dad's parents will be here, and Mom's brothers and sisters are coming and some of their kids."

Dave took a deep breath. "Mom's started cooking already. She wants to have the big freezer in the basement full so she can just defrost stuff and serve it. I'm in charge of loading and running the dishwasher every couple of hours. I get a headache just thinking about the noise. I hate holidays."

"Poor baby," I teased. I wished I were part of his family and that his mother were mine. To me, holidays should be just what Dave had described — noise and color and people talking and hugging and eating together — family doings.

"I wonder if I should at least ask Pam if she's willing to have everyone come to her house," I said, thinking out loud. "She must enjoy having people around, or she wouldn't live in such a big house. And I bet Pam's turkey will be perfectly cooked, not stuck in the oven late on high heat like Mom usually does hers."

Dave yawned with sound effects and went back to reading his comic strips as if he were bored with the subject of Thanksgiving, but I kept on going anyway, like a reel that wouldn't stop unwinding. "Maybe Pam could do the turkey and Mom could bring her ice cream pie. Everybody loves Mom's chocolate ice cream pie. I'll make the sweet-potato casserole with marshmallows and apples. That came out great last year. And Bliss can make her celery-and-cheese hors d'oeuvres."

I paused, but Dave didn't say anything, so I went on.

"Last year Avery set the table, but Pauli could do that. He needs to contribute something. And I'll make some dips and use different kinds of corn and potato chips. Not guacamole again. It turned brown when I tried it last year, and it tasted so bad even Dad wouldn't eat it. Of course, the main thing is that we all be together."

"Gilda," Dave said finally. "Does all this stuff come to you from on high? Like a voice telling you, 'This is how Thanksgiving should be'?"

"What do you mean?"

"Well, you sound as if you know everything and there's only one right way. Yours."

"Dave! That's a rotten thing to say to me."

"Yeah, I guess. But think about it sometime. Is your way the only way?"

"You rat!" I was really hurt, not just because he'd attacked me, but that he'd done it when I was already feeling low. "I'm going home."

"Don't be mad at me," he said, backing down in a hurry. "I guess I shouldn't have said anything."

"No, you shouldn't have," I told him. I liked him surprising me with kisses a lot better than with criticism.

It took him another minute to calm me down. We'd never left each other without making up, and that afternoon was no different. By the time I went home, we were friends again. I even felt safe enough to ask myself if what Dave had said about me being self-righteous had any truth in it.

But what was wrong with being the keeper of tradi-

tion? It was the turkeys and Christmas trees and birthday cakes that pulled a family together, after all —
especially a family like mine where every member took
off to do his own thing.

I found Pam's house locked. She had forgotten to give
me a key. It was a relief to discover she could goof up
occasionally, but while I sat on the front steps waiting
for her and Dad, the sun went down and it got pretty
chilly. Also, I was getting hungry even though I'd eaten
dinner at Dave's at one o'clock.

The street lamps had been lit for a while when Pam
drove up with Dad and Pauli. By then I was feeling
totally abandoned.

Pam was upset. "Oh, I'm sorry," she said. "I meant to
give you a key. Really, I'm sorry you got locked out,
Gilda. Usually I don't forget things like that."

"It's no big deal, Pam," Dad said. "I'm sure Gilda
didn't mind waiting. Did you, honey?"

What could I say? "It hasn't been that long," I lied, to
make Pam feel better.

Pauli stood on the front stoop and stretched. "Boy,
I'm tired," he said. "I'm going up to my room."

"No supper?" I asked him.

"We stopped to eat on the road," Dad said.

"Mom likes diners," Pauli said with exaggerated dis-
gust. "She always stops at some diner on our way home
from anywhere and risks getting ptomaine poisoning."

"Oh, Pauli, come off it," Pam said.

I was starving. I hoped Pam wouldn't object to my

making myself a sandwich. She handed me a key. "Here," she said. "Now be sure not to lose it, and be sure you turn off the burglar alarm when you enter the house and set it when you leave. Let me show you how it works."

Dad was watching television while Pam filled me in on operating the burglar alarm and satisfied herself that I understood how to disarm it. When I asked for permission to make myself a sandwich, Pam said, "Sure thing. Just mark down on the list by the phone anything that you finish off. I do the shopping on Thursday evenings."

"Dad doesn't mind food shopping," I said.

"I know, but he and I have it divided so that he does his half on Tuesdays on his way home from work. We're dividing household expenses equally, you understand."

"Oh, sure." I was afraid to ask her about Thanksgiving, in case it fell under more hard and fast rules.

I made myself a melted-cheese sandwich and returned to the living room to find Dad had gone to bed. Pam sat alone, writing at her desk. "Sunday nights I do my personal correspondence," she said. "I try, no matter what, to write the notes I owe friends before I go to bed."

"Do you schedule everything, Pam?"

"Well —" There was the economical smile again. "It's awful, I know, but it's the only way I can get everything done."

Dad never scheduled anything except the tennis lessons he gave, or things that other people made him do. How could he feel comfortable with a person as organized as this lady? I looked past the light surrounding Pam's desk to the darkened living room and wondered how long it would take me to feel at home here. Forever was my best guess.

I sighed and said good night and bent and kissed Pam's cheek. "Thanks for taking me in," I said.

Pam's eyes widened as if the kiss had surprised her, but then she responded with real warmth. "Why, Gilda, I'm glad to have you."

Upstairs in my bed, alone on the third floor, I decided to read until I was tired enough to fall asleep. The book was one Dave had recommended called *Walks Far Woman*, about an Indian woman who'd left her tribe and survived terrible hardships. I tried to imagine how it would feel to be cast out of my tribe and have to survive in the world alone. Wasn't I lucky that I was still being cared for even though my family had exploded into fragments? But I couldn't convince myself. No way could I make an exploded family into a minor problem. It was close to midnight before I closed the book and turned out the light.

Tomorrow I'd get Dad alone and persuade him to do Thanksgiving the right way. I could usually talk him into something that I really believed in. Then I'd ask him to take me to the mall for a new winter jacket. Clothes shopping had always been Mom's job, but Dad was the parent I was living with now. And he was going to marry Pam, I reminded myself. But I still didn't quite believe it.

11

Monday morning I got downstairs early, determined to catch Dad before he left for work. He was leaning on the counter waiting for the electric coffee maker to finish dripping through, and he looked glum.

"What's the matter?" I asked him.

"Nothing," he said, but I could see his mouth twitching the way Avery's did when he was upset.

"You don't look happy," I said.

"I'm fine, Gilda." His eyes had dark pouches under them and he didn't look like a boy anymore. I gave him a hug to comfort him, but he patted my back and said, "Listen, getting divorced's no picnic for anybody. We've just got to get through it, that's all."

I let him go. He sat down with his cup of coffee and picked up the newspaper. "Thanksgiving's this Thursday," I said gently, but not gently enough for Dad. He groaned and covered his eyes with his hand.

"Gilda," he said, when he got control of himself,

"don't bug me now, please. I'm doing my best. I know it's not good enough, but it's all I can do. You and your mother, you expect too much."

I was crushed. "*I* expect too much? Me? All I want is —"

"I know what you want, but you can't have it, okay?"

"So we're just going to skip Thanksgiving?"

"No, we're not skipping it." He hesitated as if he were trying to think, but then he just said, "Look, let's discuss this some other time."

"Tonight," I said firmly, because there wasn't going to be a turkey left to buy if we waited another day. "You can take me to the mall. I need a new winter jacket, and I need to talk to you alone."

"Okay, okay." He gave a huge sigh. "Tonight it is." He took a sip of his coffee, made a face, and said, "This machine makes terrible coffee." Then he got up and emptied his cup into the sink.

It was really hard for me to concentrate in school. I kept wondering how Avery was doing in his new class and if Bliss, who'd never been away from home before, was homesick. I kept worrying that there wouldn't be any turkeys left and that maybe Pam wouldn't let Mom come to her house for Thanksgiving.

The minute I got to Pam's after school, I called Dad at the tennis club. "Is it okay if I make a long-distance call to Bliss?" I asked.

"What about?"

"To see how she is, Dad. This is her first time away from home, you know."

"Oh, right. Sure."

Bliss didn't sound the least bit homesick. She babbled on in detail about her new piano. "Grandma even lets Cinder sit on the piano bench with me," Bliss said. And Grandma had already taken her to the zoo after the concert because it was just across the street practically. And yes, school was fine.

"Don't you miss me even a little?" I asked.

"Uh-huh," Bliss said.

I wasn't convinced. "Well," I said, "we'll see each other Thursday for Thanksgiving anyway. I'll call you about it."

"Good," Bliss said.

Next I called Avery, who sounded even more cheerful than Bliss had. "There's a kid in my class who's just like me, Gilda, except he wears thick glasses and he's kind of short and fat. But he likes Arthur C. Clarke and he's read twenty-two Asimov books."

"How many have you read?"

"Not that many. Maybe ten or twelve."

"So you've got a friend?"

"Yeah. I never had a real friend in school," Avery said.

Or in the neighborhood either, I thought. "That's great, Avery. I'm glad for you." No point in asking if he missed me. Obviously not yet.

Pauli was making spaghetti for supper. He said he liked to cook. I set the table and asked if I could do anything else to help.

"You want to make a dessert?" he asked me.

It was five o'clock. "There's time to do a cake mix if you have one."

"Look in the pantry," he said.

The pantry was stocked like a mini-supermarket. I came back with a box of brownie mix and stood beside Pauli at the counter to make it.

"You know," he said, "your dad's pretty neat."

"I think so," I said. "Usually."

"Most of the guys my mom has brought home haven't been that athletic. Like they'll ski or something, but him being a tennis pro — that's really neat."

"He's glad that you like the game. . . . He tried to coach me when I started to play, but it didn't work out."

"Why not?"

"No talent. And — I don't know. I was embarrassed to be such a dud, so I just gave it up."

"You don't do sports?" Pauli seemed surprised.

"Well, I play a little volleyball and soccer, and I swim and ride, so I'm not a couch potato exactly. I just don't compete at anything."

"My mom competed when she was in school. She was on a basketball team, and she still wins tennis trophies."

"You and she are close, aren't you?" I asked.

"Yeah, I guess."

"And you don't fight with her?" I was thinking of my mother and me.

"You kidding? Fight with the boss lady? If I tried giving her a hard time, she'd put me on bread and water in my room. No mercy." He sounded proud of it.

I confided, "My mother and I fight all the time. That's mostly how we communicate — by fighting."

"So that's why you're here instead of with her?"

"Well, also because she's only got a one-bedroom apartment. . . . And, my mother doesn't appreciate me like my dad does."

"She sounds like a witch."

"No, she's not," I said quickly. "She's got her faults, but who doesn't? She's hardworking and you can depend on her, and —" And she was my mother, and I still loved her.

"I just meant, because I heard your dad say your mother's always on his tail —" Pauli said.

"That's just a stage she's going through," I said. "You know, adults go through stages. Like right now, Mom's in a career stage, where having her own business and making money's more important than kids."

"I don't think my mom goes through stages," Pauli said.

"She's always the same?"

"Pretty much. I just wish I were smarter so I could make her proud of me, but I've never been much of a reader. She thinks I don't try, but I try. I just don't succeed."

"Like I'm not much of a tennis player," I said, because his face had clouded and I could see he felt bad about it.

"Yeah," he said and smiled.

As soon as he finished his spaghetti and meat sauce, Pauli went to turn on the TV in the living room. I stared out the kitchen window. The backyard was huge. It dipped down from a terrace to a lawn ringed by a screen of bushes and trees. It had to be gorgeous when all those bushes were in bloom. Impressive, like the house, like Pam herself, but I didn't think I'd like her as a mother. She was too much in command. A mother I couldn't fight with would cramp my style.

While we were eating Pauli's spaghetti, which was pretty spicy, I made the mistake of mentioning that Hess's had a sale. "Dad, we ought to look for my jacket there first," I said.

"You're going shopping?" Pam asked.

"Yes, Gilda and I are malling it tonight," Dad said.

"Good. How about taking Pauli?" Pam asked. "He really needs a new pair of sneakers."

Pauli groaned. "Do I have to go shopping?"

"Come on, Pauli," Dad said immediately. "It'll be okay, just you and me and Gilda." When he looked at me and saw my expression, he frowned. I stared back at him, waiting for him to remember his promise and take back the invitation to Pauli, but he didn't say a word.

"Is something wrong?" Pam asked.

"No," Dad said. "What should be wrong?"

I waited until later when I caught him alone in the hall to say, "Dad, you know it was supposed to be just us tonight."

"Ah, come on, Gilda. Don't be like that. We can still talk. The kid's not going to get in our way. And he needs bucking up."

"What about me?" I choked out. "Don't you think I have needs?"

"You?" Dad said. "Come on. You're strong enough to carry us all."

I stood there openmouthed and speechless. Usually I'm proud of being strong, but it was working against me now. I went to the bathroom to put myself back together. No matter what, I had to get Thanksgiving settled tonight. Pauli could look for his sneakers, but Dad and I had to talk.

I got to the car and found Pauli sitting in the front seat next to Dad. They were deep into a discussion about wide-bodied tennis racquets. All the way to the mall, they rattled on nonstop about tennis equipment. I could have killed them both.

"Come to Hess's with me, Dad," I commanded when we got out of the car. "Pauli can buy his own sneakers."

"Oh, now, Gilda," Dad coaxed, "it won't take long to get his sneaks. If you don't want to wait, you go ahead, and we'll meet you in the coat department after you've picked out what you want."

I glared at him, telling him with my eyes what I thought of that.

"Honey, you know I'm not much on female fashions."

"I need to *talk* to you," I said. "Thanksgiving's *Thursday*. And it's already Monday night."

"You know who you sound like? Your mother."

"Thanks a bunch," I snapped. Then I turned my back on him and on Pauli, who was hunched over pretending to examine his sneakers, and I marched off toward Hess's. For years I've been pushing for the right to shop for myself. Why did I have to get it just when I didn't want it? Dad had broken his promise. I was angry and hurt, too. I missed Bliss and Avery. This whole divorce thing was ripping a hole in my chest.

Nothing Hess's had in my size appealed to me. I waited at the entrance of the store a good hour before Dad and Pauli came ambling back. Pauli was swinging a plastic bag from the shoe store. "So," Dad said, "did you find what you wanted?"

"Not here."

"Where do you want to go then? We're all yours."

I shrugged. "I don't know. Maybe I'll get Mom to take me sometime."

Instead of acting guilty, all Dad said to that was, "Okay, then how about some ice cream? Pauli and I have a yen for chocolate sundaes."

"Dad!" I reproached him. "You know I can't eat ice cream when I just had a brownie for dessert. You want me to get fat?"

"So have a cone instead of a sundae." He was smiling amiably, too busy playing big daddy to Pauli to be anything to me.

"Maybe I'll keep looking for a jacket and meet you after," I said. I knew the long-suffering martyr was a miserable role, but I was too angry at Dad to stop playing it.

"Fine," he said as if he believed I really wanted to shop alone. "We'll see you in an hour by the entrance where we parked. Will that give you time enough?" He sounded so innocent that I couldn't tell whether he didn't realize that I was angry at him for not paying attention to me, or whether he realized it but refused to feel guilty about it.

I nodded and walked away from them. I had a headache. I couldn't remember when I'd felt so rotten.

Grimly I cruised through the mall, shopping any store that had jackets. Nothing seemed right to me. In a full-length mirror I saw a large girl with dark, angry eyes. That's me, I realized, and I tried to make the anger disappear. What was left was sadness. Dad was too busy wooing the new kid to pay attention to his own daughter's needs. How did I get stuck with such a self-centered family? I'd be better off just loving Dave and Fettucini and my girlfriends. At least they loved me back.

"So," Dad said when we reconnected at the entrance, "find anything?"

"No. Did you and Pauli have fun?"

"We did." Dad draped an arm over Pauli's shoulder as if they'd become best buddies. Pauli's grin made me seethe.

"Dad," I burst out, "if you don't make time to talk to me tonight, I'll never forgive you."

"What are you so mad about?" he asked. "I'm here. Talk to me."

"Alone," I snarled.

"All right, honey," he said, Mr. Meek himself.

This time he was true to his word. At the house, he told Pauli he'd see him later, that he was going for a walk with his daughter. But under the first street lamp, he said, "Listen, Gilda, I can't afford to turn the boy off. It's important that he and I get along."

"Besides," I said bitterly, "you're thrilled to finally get a kid who's a tennis player."

"Don't be like that. Come on. You know I hate disappointing you, but Pauli's never had a father, and you've got a full set of parents."

"Not anymore I don't."

He gave me a reproving glance, and we walked in silence until the next lamppost, which was in front of a house even bigger and older-looking than Pam's. There Dad started chatting, as if that would cool me down. "Pam says there's just one little old lady living alone in this place. Would you want to float around by yourself in a house this big?"

"Not me," I said. "I'd fill it up with people." But then I ran out of patience and plunged right in. "Dad, about Thanksgiving, could you ask Pam if she'll have it at her house and invite Mom and Avery and Bliss?"

"You kidding?"

"Why should I be kidding?"

"You expect Pam to invite your mother for dinner? No way. Besides, Pam's promised to go to her sister's in Syracuse. That's where most of her family live now."

"Oh, well, if she's leaving, maybe she'll let us use her house. Then we could have Mom and that would work out fine."

"Except — Gilda, did I forget to tell you? I'm going with her. She wants me to meet her family."

It took me a while to catch my breath, and then I burst out with, "What about *your* family, Dad?"

"You're supposed to come, too."

"And Bliss and Avery and Mom?"

"Bliss is with Grandma in New York, and your mother mentioned something to me about having

Thanksgiving dinner with her support group. She's taking Avery."

"When did she tell you that?"

"I don't know. A few days ago."

I groaned.

"What's the matter?"

"We aren't even going to be together on the biggest family holiday of the year? What do you *mean* what's the matter?" I cried. "What's the matter with *you*, Dad?" I turned and ran back to Pam's house. I knew why Mom hadn't told me about the support group dinner. She'd been afraid I'd give her a hard time about it. And she was so right.

Later, Dad knocked on my bedroom door. "Gilda, please honey," he begged. "Don't do this to me. Come out. Come on. You know I love you."

I put my pillow over my head so that I couldn't hear him. He was as bad as Mom. They were both too selfish to care about their children's needs, unless it was something material and unimportant like a new winter jacket. Emotional needs didn't count. Or maybe it was just *children's* emotional needs that didn't count with them.

12

The tailfeathers had been torn off the Thanksgiving display turkey at school. I saw the long colored strips giving thanks for world peace, a baby sister, a new bike, scattered on the floor in front of the bulletin board. What do kids get out of vandalism like that? Am I the only one who thinks it's a great holiday?

I'd promised Bliss and Avery we'd be together for Thanksgiving. But I walked to my homeroom thinking that the only way I could pull that off now was to talk Mom into inviting Grandma and Bliss up here to her group dinner. Then I'd ask Dad to join us for at least half the day before he went to Pam's party. We were his only blood relatives, after all — Grandma and Bliss and Avery and me.

Or should I first talk to Grandma and persuade her to make the trip? It was hard imagining Grandma among a bunch of single parents with kids running all over the place. She'd probably stiffen up and act snooty. Well, eating with a group of strangers wasn't how I pictured Thanksgiving either. If Grandma wouldn't come, maybe I could go down on the train and bring Bliss back myself. It was so complicated. And I only had a day and a half to arrange it.

Suddenly I found myself lost in a maze of details, like if Grandma came, she'd insist on brussels sprouts and chestnuts because that was a tradition in her family. Well, if she wanted brussels sprouts and chestnuts, she'd have to make the dish herself. She's the only one who likes them anyway. Which meant we'd better have something everyone did like, like corn. A corn pudding would be good.

At lunch, I asked Bebe and Jane and Stephanie what they ate on Thanksgiving. "Mom makes a ham," Steph said. "Everybody in our family despises turkey."

"We have the works," Bebe said. "Turkey and stuffing and cranberry mold and baked potatoes and six different kinds of vegetables, and pumpkin pie and a cream cake."

"A cream cake after all that?" Steph said. "Yuck."

"The cream cake's my favorite part," Bebe protested. "We always have one, usually chocolate."

"Well, for your information, cream cake's not traditional, Bebe," Jane said. "Traditional desserts should be pumpkin pie and mince pie."

"Mince pie! Ugh, sick!" Bebe said.

I suspected Dave was the one at our table who'd have the most traditional menu, but he wasn't paying attention to the conversation. He sat quietly eating a hot dog and reviewing vocabulary for the quiz we were going to have that afternoon.

"Efficacious" he said. "What's a good sentence for 'efficacious'?"

"'I'd like to think of an efficacious way to bring my family together for Thanksgiving,'" I said.

Instead of waiting until Mom got to her apartment that evening, I called her at work from Pam's house after school. "How many people can you bring to that dinner your support group's giving, Mom?"

"Why?" Mom asked. "You don't want to come, do you, Gilda?"

"Not really. What I'd like is for our family to have a dinner by ourselves," I said.

Instantly, Mom went on the defensive. "Well, there's no way we can do that this year. But you kids are all welcome at the support group dinner. I'm definitely going to it. These people have been good friends to me, and I need them more than ever now."

"Can Grandma and Dad come if they want?"

"You're kidding. Your *grandmother?*" Mom hesitated, then said slowly. "Well, I can't imagine — but I guess if she wanted to. We just have to bring enough food to cover everybody. But the deadline for reservations is tonight, so you'd better find out the head count soon. Oh, and Gilda, if you're coming, how about cooking that potato thing you made last year that everybody liked?"

"Sure." I was pleased that Mom remembered. "Mom, you wouldn't want to call Grandma for me, would you?"

"*Me?* Call the frost queen? You've got to be kidding. . . . Listen, I have to go. Anything else on your mind?"

"That's it," I said.

"Gilda . . ." She hesitated. "Listen, don't turn this against me now, but I want to tell you — I appreciate how hard this is on you, I mean the divorce. Believe me, if I could have stuck it out with your father until you grew up, I would have for your sake."

"Mom!" I gasped, but she cut me off before I could catch my breath.

"That's all I have to say. I don't want to discuss it further. 'Bye now," she said, and the phone went dead.

I sat there and cried for a minute, until I realized nothing was going to change even if Mom did feel bad about what she was doing to me. We were still getting divorced, and I still had to arrange Thanksgiving. I dried my eyes and got back to work.

At a minute after five, I called New York City, because that's when the phone rates get cheaper — but it still left time to talk before Pam and Dad got home from work. I didn't want them to hear my conversation with Grandma in case it didn't go right.

"Grandma," I began. "You know what a major family holiday Thanksgiving is?"

"Yes, Gilda. I'm aware of its importance. Certainly I am," Grandma said.

"Well, would you be willing to do me a big favor so we could all be together for it?"

"What kind of a big favor?"

"Come up here with Bliss and go with us to a special

dinner Mom's signed up for. . . . It's sort of a community Thanksgiving meal."

"What do you mean? A community meal?" Grandma sounded suspicious. "Thanksgiving should be in your own home. I wouldn't think of going out to be served dry turkey smothered in some dreadful thick gravy."

"But Mom's place is too small to have us all there," I said, avoiding the truth that Mom apparently hadn't even considered the possibility, "and she has these friends in her support group who want to share —"

"Friends? Support group? What do you mean, Gilda? Has your mother joined some kind of commune?"

"No, it's a support group for divorced people."

Grandma's gasp said it for her. "I am certainly not dragging Bliss upstate to expose her to such a thing," Grandma said. "If you want, tell your mother that I'll do Thanksgiving here in my apartment, and you and Avery and your parents can come to us. You're old enough to help me, and I'm sure I did the dinner for enough years to remember how it goes. I'll even make my mother's recipe for brussels sprouts and chestnuts. I can cook and peel the chestnuts ahead of time. Yes, and we'll just buy the pies —"

"Grandma," I interrupted her.

"What?"

"Thank you. You're the only one in the family who cares. Thank you. I love you," I said. I would even eat a full portion of the brussels sprouts and chestnuts to please her.

Pam came in from work a while later and found me

sitting in the kitchen surrounded by her cookbooks.

"What are you up to?" she asked as she slipped out of her suit jacket and poured herself a glass of grapefruit juice.

"Planning our Thanksgiving feast," I said happily. "Dad's mother's going to have it in New York."

"Is she? For whom?"

"For me and Bliss and Avery and Mom and Dad."

If Pam was surprised, she hid it well. She still looked bright and interested when she said, "I was hoping you'd come with your father and Pauli and me to my family in Syracuse, Gilda."

"Well, that would be nice," I said as politely as I could. "I mean, I'm sure you have a nice family and — but Thanksgiving should be your own family. . . . Besides, my mother and grandmother couldn't go to Syracuse, too, and Grandma'd be hurt if she got left out."

Pam shook her head. "That's the trouble with these family holidays. The logistics are mind-boggling. And believe me, Gilda, they never turn out to be the fun you expect."

"Yes they do," I protested. The one time I could expect my parents and brother and sister to follow the script was Thanksgiving, Christmas, and birthdays. Well, sometimes not on birthdays. Bliss had thrown a fit and cried all through her seventh birthday because she hadn't gotten a cat. And Avery had had pneumonia and nearly died on his last birthday.

"You mean," Pam insisted, "you *like* eating too much and trying to have a conversation with somebody you haven't seen in a year while the football game is on?"

"I like everybody being together and sharing. And I like all the food and excitement."

Dad walked in then. Pam said to him, "Well, it looks as if you have a choice, Skip. You can come to Syracuse with me as planned, or go to New York for a bang-up Thanksgiving with your just-about-to-be-exed wife and your kids. Courtesy of —" Pam flipped her hand open at me in a gesture that showed her annoyance.

"Grandma's willing to have us all," I told Dad. "She's the only one who is."

"Yikes," Dad groaned. "What did I walk into now?"

Later he asked me if I had spoken to Mom about it. "Not yet," I admitted.

"Talk to her, then, and see what she says. I can't believe she'd be willing to go down to your grandmother's."

He was right. There was a silence on the phone line after I told Mom about the Thanksgiving party in New York. What she finally said echoed Pam's remarks. "Listen, I've never understood what's so great about working yourself to a state of exhaustion so you can make yourself sick from overeating. If it means so much to you, Gilda, get your father to take you and Avery down there. I'm not going."

"Even for your children's sake?"

"There you go making me feel like a bum just because —"

"But it's *Thanksgiving*, Mom. Instead of a made-up family, wouldn't your real one be better?"

Mom raised her voice. "Don't you lay that guilt trip

on me, Gilda. I'm *not* going to your grandmother's. Make her come here if it's so important to you."

I asked to speak to Avery. "I don't care," he said when I questioned him. "Whatever you want is okay with me."

"But you think it's important for us to be together, don't you?"

"I guess so," he said. "Could we go by train? I've never been on the train."

"Sure," I promised him. "If it's just you and me, we'll have to go by train."

The second long-distance phone call to New York had better come out of my allowance, I decided. Two calls in one evening was taking unfair advantage. "Yes?" Grandma sounded as chilly as if she expected to be sold something.

"It's me, Grandma. It looks like I'll be coming down with just Avery and not Mom. Dad's still not coming either. He's going to Pam's family."

"Oh, is that so? Where is that son of mine? I want to speak to him."

Hope leaped inside me at Grandma's forceful tone, but in the end it turned out that either Pam was stronger than Grandma or Dad was still rebelling against her. He wouldn't go.

Dad told me that Grandma would meet Avery and me when we got off the train in Grand Central Station. "I hope this isn't going to be too much for her," he said to me. "She's not as young as she used to be."

"We can keep the dinner simple," I said. "So long as there's turkey and we eat it together."

"I know. I know. You've made everything very clear. Your parents have failed you. We're not the ideal family. Well —" He pressed his lips together. "I'm sorry, Gilda. I did try. I married your mother, and we had you kids with the best of intentions, but it didn't work out. What can I say?" He shrugged, as if what had happened were no fault of his.

"Dad, when you bring a baby into the world, shouldn't you put the child first, before what you want for yourself?" I asked him.

He looked uncomfortable. "What are you saying? That I'm not a responsible father?"

"No, but —" What I was accusing him of was hard to put into words. "You do what you want. Like, you wouldn't give up being a tennis pro to help Mom. You jog. You see your friends. Maybe if you'd been willing to help her more —"

"No," he said. "Your mother just got sick of being a mother. We got married too young, and she thought it would be easy, but it wasn't. And then she started thinking about what a big shot she could be if she hadn't latched onto me. And then she decided she'd better start making it before she got any older."

His voice took on a pleading tone. "I haven't changed, Gilda. I'm the same easygoing slob your mother fell for when we were seventeen. Now maybe you think that's not enough, but that's who I am. Your grandmother was never satisfied with me either. She wanted me to be a hotshot lawyer like my father. Well, I like to hit tennis balls, and I'm a pretty good teacher, and I like my life the way it is." He looked as if where he found himself at the end of his speech surprised him.

"Anyway," he said, "Pam thinks I'm okay. She likes me."

"I like you too," I said, to appease him. And I did love him even though he was self-centered. Maybe I was wrong about family. Maybe I was crazy to think that children should be cared for and that their needs mattered most. It could be that kids existed just to please their parents. It could be it was everybody for himself, sink or swim, in this world. That's how it seemed to work in my family anyway.

13

Seeing the snow flurries Wednesday, the day before Thanksgiving, I put on my duffle coat. I'd planned to wear my good white spring jacket to look nice in the city, but the duffle coat was warmer. Mom would have hated seeing me go off to Grandma's in that shabby coat. Even Pam frowned when she saw me in it, but she didn't say anything except, "Have fun in New York." Then she tucked a twenty-dollar bill into my pocket.

"I can't take that," I protested.

"Gilda, don't insult me by refusing to accept a gift from me, or I really will think you don't like me."

"I do like you," I said.

"Good. Then keep the money. I'm sorry you're not spending the holiday with your dad and me," Pam said, "but I do understand why you want to go to your grandmother's. Maybe next year we'll work something out here."

"Maybe," I said, to be polite. Then I thanked her for the money and wished her a happy Thanksgiving.

Dad tried to give me more money. "In case you need to take a taxi," he said. "Even bus transportation will cost you plenty in the city if the three of you go anywhere alone."

"Thanks, but Pam took care of it," I told him. I showed him the twenty.

"That's from her," he said stubbornly. "This is from me. Listen, babe, you are my first best daughter, and I do love you a lot and want to be with you."

"I know, Dad. It's okay. I'm not mad at you."

I wasn't mad at either of my parents anymore. I'd decided they couldn't help being a little immature, which was what made them more concerned about their own needs than their kids'. It wouldn't help to blame them. But someone in our family had better put kids first, and I was the only one left to do it.

Even without parents, I was looking forward to the long weekend because I really missed my brother and sister.

I took the two small bags I'd packed to school with me. Dave let me stow one in his locker. Mom was supposed to pick up Avery, and then me, at noon when school let out, and drive us to the train station.

"So," Dave said after we managed to squeeze our locker doors shut on the extra baggage, "what're you going to do down in the big city?"

"Eat a lot of beautiful crisp-skinned turkey and stuffing and cranberry sauce and so forth and so on," I said. "Avery and Bliss and Grandma and I are going to do it up right even if my parents don't think it's important."

Dave made a face.

"What's the matter with you?" I asked.

"It seems to me you're making too big a thing of this, Gilda. I mean, it's like you're trying to show up your folks or something."

"Well, I am going to show them that if *they* don't want to bother making a real Thanksgiving for their children, *we* can do it for ourselves." I glared at him. "Why are you so critical of me lately?"

"I don't know. I guess I just don't think your parents are so bad. I like them."

"So do I," I said. It annoyed me that Dave didn't appreciate what I was doing and how hard it was for me. Praise and encouragement were what I needed from him now, not criticism. To show him how hurt I was, I avoided him the rest of the morning.

"Happy turkey," Dave said when he handed me my bag from his locker at noon.

"You too," was my only reply. Then I marched outside to wait for my mother to pick me up. It would serve Dave right to have to wait until Monday when I came back to school to make peace with me.

If Mom noticed my jacket, she didn't say anything about it. That surprised me, especially since she'd bought Avery a new bomber jacket. He looked older in it. "Wow, don't you look cool!" I said.

Avery grinned and ducked his head.

Mom climbed aboard the train with us and saw to it we were seated facing each other on the river view side of the aisle. She kissed Avery good-bye, looked at me warily, and said, "How about a kiss, Gilda?"

I kissed her. Awkwardly Mom said, "Well, so, this is what you want. You have a good time now."

"You too, Mom," I said.

She hung onto my hand for a few seconds too long. Finally she squeezed it and said, "How about we have lunch next Saturday, and you can tell me all about your weekend in New York. Actually, I'd like to hear about *everything* that's going on in your life."

"Sure," I said. "That'd be great." Lunch! Mom must be seeing me as an adult already. Well, doing lunch together was better than fighting. I tucked her invitation into the back of my mind to enjoy later.

Once we were alone, Avery seemed shy with me. I told him about the ruined castle on the Hudson that we were going to pass. "The guy that built it never lived in it," I said. "It looks like a real castle. . . . Av, when did Mom buy you the jacket?"

"She brought it home last night. My arms stuck way out of my old one." He was staring out the window as if he were afraid of missing something.

"Relax, the castle doesn't come up for an hour, or maybe two," I said. "You look tough in that jacket, Av. You look . . . neat."

He smiled at me. "They don't pick on me in the new school. Yet."

"How're the teachers?"

"Okay. School's good so long as nobody's booby-trapping my locker and sticking my head in toilets."

"Yeah, I see what you mean. But if you'd told me, I could probably have done something for you."

He shrugged. "You couldn't have stopped them. . . . Do you want to see the new story I'm writing?"

"Sure."

"It's not typed. Want me to read it to you?"

"You bet." Avery's printed letters ran into each other in a scrawly mess that was hard to read.

We almost missed the castle after all, because his story filled two notebooks. It was mostly about a star-ship that kept getting into trouble in space. First it was bombarded by space crystals that coated its wings and sent it off course into a hostile galaxy where warring tribes were destroying their solar systems. Then it was sucked into a black hole. The hero emerged from that transformed into a photoelectic worm.

"So what do you think?" Avery asked anxiously at the end of the second notebook but not the story. He hadn't decided how to end it yet.

"I think you're amazing. Where do you find the time to write all that stuff?"

"I don't know. I keep a notebook with me, and I write in it when I get an idea. My math teacher made me check it with him at the beginning of class, but he gave it back to me because I handed my work in early, so it worked out okay."

"And what will you do when you finish the story?"

"Think up another one, I guess."

"Maybe you'll be a writer instead of a scientist some-day, Av."

"Yeah," Avery said. "Probably I'll do something like that. What'll you do, Gilda?"

I was surprised. He didn't often ask me questions about myself. What would I do? "Get married and have children," I said. "If I can find the right guy."

"You're just going to be a wife and mother?"

"Well, I'll probably also need to work at something that pays a salary, but I don't know what. It doesn't matter, just so long as I can make my own hours and get home in time to be with the kids."

"I don't want kids," Avery said. "I'm gonna be a bachelor."

"How come?"

"There's too much fighting with kids. I like it quiet."

"Well, I'll invite you over to my house if you get lonely."

"Okay," he said. "I'll come."

I smiled and asked him what he wanted to do in the city. "We could go to the Museum of Natural History," I suggested. "That's on the other side of the park from where Grandma is."

"And the zoo," Avery said. "Bliss says the zoo's across the street."

"You spoke to her?"

"Yeah, Grandma called and put Bliss on."

"Long distance?" I said. "Boy, Grandma's changed!"

"She says it's a shame," Avery said. "She says that you're the only one that cares about the family, and nobody helps you."

I was pleased to hear that Grandma appreciated me even if Dave didn't.

"Mom was mad when Grandma finished talking to

144

her," Avery went on. "She said Grandma wasn't that great a mother herself."

"I guess being a good mother's really hard." I said it, but in my heart I knew it would be a cinch for me.

"Being a kid's hard, too," Avery said.

I nodded. "You can say that again. Everything we want, we have to ask an adult for, and they can always say no. They're the generals. We're just the troops."

But I couldn't help smiling. The closer we got to the city, the more confident I was that this would be a Thanksgiving my brother and sister and I would always remember.

14

Grandma looked old but sort of well polished as she stood on the platform, waiting for Avery and me to come to her. Her narrow eyes and thin mouth were sunk in wrinkles, and she was too pale, but her gray hair was styled like Mom's, and her fur-trimmed coat fitted her just so.

Bliss came racing down the platform toward us yelling, "Gilda! Gilda!" as if we'd been separated for months instead of days.

I caught her in my arms and hugged her hard. "I'm so glad to see you, Bliss."

"Me too," Bliss said. "But Grandma's not feeling good."

"I'm fine," Grandma said when we reached her and I asked her what was wrong. She offered me a cheek to kiss and turned to Avery. "You can kiss me; I'm not infectious." Avery looked scared, but he dutifully touched his lips to Grandma's cheek. She slipped her arm through mine and said, "Let's find a taxi and get home."

She had to lean on me as she led us through the station. Once she halted and wavered as if she might fall. "You're really sick, Grandma," I said in alarm.

"Vertigo. That's all it is. I've had bouts like this before. I just need to get home to bed."

With me supporting her on one side and Avery and Bliss on the other, Grandma made it into a taxi. At her apartment house, the doorman helped her into the elevator, clucking over her in concern.

"Not necessary," she told him when he asked if he should call her doctor. "I'll be fine as soon as I'm in my own bed."

After we'd walked Grandma into her bedroom, I asked if she needed help getting undressed. "Certainly not!" Grandma said. "Go be with your sister and brother, and let me sleep. I'll take a pill and be fine soon."

Once, when I was Bliss's age, I'd gone down to New York with Dad when he had an interview for a new job. The job hadn't worked out, and Mom had given him a hard time about that as I remember. I also remember that when I'd enthused to Mom about all the beautiful things on the lit glass shelves of Grandma's living room cabinet — the jade horse and the enameled coach and the ivory Chinese lady — Mom had said, "Sure, she's got a lot of nice stuff because your grandpa made a lot of money, but *you'll* never see any of it. When your father didn't measure up, she decided to leave all her money to your grandpa's old college. It's already in her will."

"Mother's got a right to leave her money where she thinks it will do the most good," Dad had argued.

"But you're her only child. That should count for something," Mom had said. When he shrugged, she added, "What really cooked your goose was that you married me after she warned you not to."

During Grandma's annual visits to our house, she and Mom were polite to each other on the surface, but I always knew they didn't like each other.

In Grandma's long narrow living room, everything still looked green in the dim light, and the curios in the lighted cabinet were still in the same place. But I couldn't remember what had stood in the foyer where Bliss's piano was now. "How are the piano lessons going?" I asked Bliss.

"Good. My teacher used to play at Carnegie Hall. Grandma takes me to her studio in a taxi."

"Really? You're lucky."

Cinder was coiled on a cushion on the piano bench. While I scratched behind her ear she yawned at me, as relaxed as if she had always lived in Grandma's apartment.

Avery asked where the TV was. Bliss opened the doors of a low cabinet, where a TV and a VCR were hidden. Avery began searching through a TV guide for his show.

"Are you happy here with Grandma, Bliss?" I asked.

"Uh-huh. Want me to play you the piece I'm practicing?"

"Not while Grandma's trying to sleep. . . . You don't miss us even a little?"

"Oh, yes, I miss you, Gilda, but — Grandma's really nice to me. We go to the zoo and we talk, and she keeps banana ice cream in the freezer for me, and —" Bliss stopped and looked at me, her pretty face big-eyed with guilt. "Umm," she said uncertainly.

I had to smile. "It's okay, Bliss. I can see why you like it here."

"I practice my piano every day," Bliss said. "Grandma doesn't mind, and I'm doing good in school, too."

"You always do well in school." And why not? Bliss liked orderly, predictable things like schoolwork and Grandma's apartment. Me, I'd hate living with Grandma, but for Bliss it was ideal.

My spirits sank. I told myself I must be tired. Usually if I felt down it was because I was tired. Or hungry. That was it. I was hungry. "Is Grandma going to give us anything to eat tonight?" I asked.

"She was going to take us out for dinner," Bliss said. "But we can't go without her. I'm not allowed to leave the apartment house alone except to go to school. That's what I don't like most about New York."

I was glad there was something she didn't like. "Well, let's see what's in the refrigerator," I said.

Stuffed in it were the ingredients for Thanksgiving dinner: a turkey that barely fit and, of course, the brussels sprouts and a container of cooked and peeled chestnuts. By unloading most of the food in front, I located an unopened package of cheddar cheese. I made us all melted-cheese sandwiches. Then I went to find out if Grandma wanted anything to eat, but she was asleep. I closed the door quietly and tiptoed away. Grandma had said she'd feel fine when she woke up. I certainly hoped so.

"What's your school like?" I asked Bliss.

"It's nice. A van picks me up in the morning. There's only twelve girls in my English class and no boys. And we have to write every day and correct each other's work."

Bliss put her finger to her lip thoughtfully, in a gesture that made me think of Grandma, and added, "I hate reading aloud, though. The first day I whispered, but today my voice came out." Excitedly she confided, "And I might get invited to a birthday party. I might, maybe. This girl said. Her name is Susan. She's not from here either."

"Good," I said. Bliss had never had many friends, and never more than one at a time. Since her best friend had moved away last summer, she'd been alone a lot. "I'm glad you've made friends, Bliss."

"Just one friend so far. Just Susan."

At night in the darkened apartment with Avery sleeping on the couch in the living room and me sharing Bliss's bed in the spare room, I felt blue again. Tired, I tried to tell myself. But it worried me that Bliss was so contented in New York. What if our fragmented family never did get back together? What if each of us stayed where we'd landed? Avery and Bliss, Dad and Mom, even Cinder, fitted pretty comfortably into their separate niches. It seemed I was the only one who wanted to have the family whole. Because a whole family is beautiful, I told myself, the way a patchwork quilt is beautiful for its total pattern even if the individual pieces are plain.

My tears caught me by surprise. Don't be a baby, I scolded myself. Tomorrow's Thanksgiving, and it will be fine.

15

In the morning I saw Grandma coming out of the bathroom. She looked awfully pasty and shriveled. "Want me to call your doctor?" I asked her anxiously.

"No. Sometimes this vertigo takes more than a day to go away. I hope this isn't going to be a long bout." She leaned against the door. "Order up something already prepared from the market, Gilda. They have good roast beef and potato salad — or whatever you want. Their number's on the pad by the phone there. Tell them to deliver. I'm sorry about Thanksgiving dinner." She looked sorry as she returned to her room.

Since it was a holiday, I wasn't surprised that the market didn't answer when I called them. Well, we had plenty of food in the refrigerator. I'd just cook our Thanksgiving dinner myself. The first thing to deal with was the turkey. I lugged it to the sink, slit the heavy plastic wrapping with a knife and peeled it off. Turning on the oven to preheat wasn't difficult, but I couldn't find a pan in Grandma's overstuffed kitchen cabinets big enough for the turkey. Bliss finally came up with some disposable aluminum roasting pans.

"That must be what she bought to use," I said. I washed the turkey, but I wasn't sure how to stuff it, so I just plunked it in one of the pans.

Avery located the spice shelf for me. "Do we have to have turkey?" he asked.

"Of course we do," I assured him. "Everything's going to be just like it should be. You'll see." I sprinkled on salt and pepper, and was considering whether to try the oregano, when I smelled something burning. Smoke was seeping from the oven. Flames shot out the minute I pulled down the oven door. Bliss screamed and I slammed the door shut. After shutting off the gas, I filled a pot with water, opened the door again, and threw water at the flames.

"I'll call the fire department," Avery said. "Where's the phone?"

"Don't," I said. "It's just paper. Grandma must have kept paper bags in the oven. I should have looked."

In a few minutes the fire was out, but the oven was a soggy mess. I set to work cleaning it out.

An hour later, I finally got the oven back on and started cooking the turkey. Bliss found the largest cooking pot Grandma owned for the sweet potatoes. They'd have to cook on top of the stove since the oven was so small that the turkey filled it. I covered the potatoes with water. After they were boiled, I'd mash them up with some sugar and butter and a can of pineapple that

I spotted on Grandma's one-shelf pantry. It would be sort of like the candied baked sweet potatoes I'd done last year — I hoped.

Bliss complained about being hungry, so while the potatoes were cooking, I looked for cereal for a late breakfast. Of course Grandma had nothing easy like dry cereal, just oatmeal. I put some in another pot to cook on the stove, and set Bliss and Avery to looking for the milk and sugar we needed. When they couldn't find any, I joined them in the search, and the minute I had my back turned, the oatmeal boiled over. What wasn't stuck to the stove burners was stuck to the pan.

By the time I'd cleaned that up, and we'd each eaten a small bowl of lumpy oatmeal with Karo syrup and the milk that Avery had discovered way back in the refrigerator, the sweet potato pot began to boil over, too.

"Oh, no!" Bliss said. "Let's stop cooking, Gilda. Let's forget Thanksgiving."

I bit my lip in frustration. "I can cook fine at home, where I know where everything is," I said. The sweet potatoes were an unappealing mush. I considered fishing out the skins and mixing the rest with butter and syrup and calling that sweet potato pudding, but I could see by Bliss's and Avery's faces that they weren't going to eat any no matter what I called it.

I checked the oven. It didn't seem very hot, and the turkey still looked white and raw.

My stomach rumbled. The oatmeal hadn't filled me up. I was exhausted and hungry, and it was already noon. My brother's and sister's glum faces made me lose confidence. Dragging Avery down here so we could be with Bliss had been my idea after all. Jokingly I asked, "Do they have a cafeteria in the zoo?"

"Yes," Bliss said. "Oh, let's go there, Gilda. Let's."

"Yeah," Avery said with enthusiasm, "let's go to the zoo."

I straightened up. "But we've got to get this meal together."

"Why?" Avery asked. "We could pretend we're on another planet where it's not Thanksgiving. Let's stop cooking and go to the zoo. Please, Gilda."

I swallowed hard and looked at Bliss, who asked, "Is it going to be ready soon?"

"The turkey? Probably not for hours."

"I don't think Grandma'll want to eat any," Bliss said.

Suddenly I collapsed. Sitting on the floor, I hit my fists against the stove and wailed. It seemed that even the oven was against me. I had fought so hard and long for this Thanksgiving! I had stood up to my parents, persuaded my brother and sister, even convinced my *grandmother* to help, and still nothing was working out. I was infuriated that I couldn't make it happen.

As frustrated and miserable as I felt, I was only vaguely aware of Bliss hugging me from one side and Avery patting my back on the other.

"What's all the noise about?" Grandma asked. She had appeared like a ghost in the doorway.

"The turkey didn't cook and Gilda feels bad," Avery told her.

Grandma put her fingers to her head and seemed

about to faint. In alarm, I said, "It's okay. I'm all right now. You'd better go back to bed." I got up to help her, but she waved me away and stumbled off to her room by herself.

Avery and Bliss were staring at me with such worried expressions that I forced the corners of my lips up in an imitation smile, even though what I wanted to do most was pound the stove and scream some more. "You know what?" I said. "We'll make Grandma a cup of tea and tell her we're going to the zoo. The heck with it."

I turned off the oven. It was an admission of total defeat, but it was what my brother and sister wanted. I just hoped the zoo cafeteria wasn't closed for the holiday.

Grandma poked her head up off the pillow when I brought her the tea. "I'm feeling better," she croaked. "Another few hours and it'll be over. Let's hold Thanksgiving until tomorrow, shall we?"

"Don't worry about it. I'm taking the kids to the zoo, Grandma."

"You are? Oh. . . . Well, all right, Gilda, but where's my pocketbook? You'll need money."

I told her I had plenty.

Grandma groaned and promised, "I'll make it up to you tomorrow." She lay back down without even touching her tea. I asked if she wanted anything. "No, no, just go. But be careful," she said. "New York's not safe for children. I'm so sorry, Gilda. You're such a good girl. I meant to do right by you."

A cold wind was blowing. I took Bliss's and Avery's hands at the corner. When the light turned green, we crossed Fifth Avenue together and walked the few blocks to Sixty-fourth Street and the zoo. Behind the waist-high stone wall in Central Park, the leafless skeletons of trees swayed and creaked in the wind. They fitted my mood. I wanted to groan and swing my arms about, too. Instead I listened to Bliss chatter on about the Delacorte clock.

The clock was outside the zoo and striking the hour musically as we arrived.

"See the kangaroo with the baby in her pouch?" Bliss asked in delight. Together with half a dozen other people, we stood looking up as the animal figures revolved, each playing a different instrument. Avery claimed the best one was the hippo playing a violin.

"What's your favorite, Gilda?" Bliss asked.

"They're all wonderful," I said with a fake enthusiasm that Bliss didn't question.

I paid the entrance fee from my first twenty, and Bliss marched us to the seal pool. So few people were standing around that we could get right up close. Probably everybody is busy cooking or eating their Thanksgiving feasts, I thought regretfully — not that my brother and sister seemed to care. Their faces glowed as they watched two jet-propelled seals racing each other through the water. Avery rested his elbows on the railing, prepared to stay there indefinitely.

Bouncing with excitement, Bliss urged us on toward the tropical jungle. "It's warm in there, and it's my favorite," she said. "Except for the polar bears. There's a polar bear that likes me. He kissed me through the glass."

"Bliss, don't be dumb," Avery said.

"No, he did, really. He looked right at me and pushed his nose against the glass."

"He probably wanted to eat you," Avery said.

"He didn't, Avery. He really —"

"Come on," I interrupted. "Let's go check out this jungle."

Bliss skipped ahead of us, but she stopped beside the room-sized glass cage at the entrance to the building. She and Avery watched two big black toucans rubbing their enormous yellow bills against each other. I watched the toucans, too, wondering if Dad and Mom were doing any better with their Thanksgivings than I was.

Inside the building, I was amazed to find myself suddenly walking on a boardwalk through the warm, humid air of a rain forest. Exotic birds in vivid colors flew through hanging vines and broad-leafed trees overhead. The sense of being magically transported to a real jungle relieved some of my bitterness.

"I like the fairy bluebird," Bliss said, "because I like its name."

Avery was taken with a piranha display called "School of Ill Repute." "I didn't know they were so big," he said.

He was right. Those fish were as big as dinner plates. "Yeah, imagine being chomped on by them," I said.

Bliss shuddered. Avery laughed. I dragged myself after them past the tortoises and turtles and alligators. I agreed with Avery that, yes, the leaf-cutting ants carrying green leaf umbrellas up the hill to their underground labyrinth were fascinating, but I was still too disappointed to *feel* fascinated.

The bats drew me. Their black shapes seemed so sad and strange as they wheeled about in a darkened glass room made to look like a cave. But Bliss took my hand and pulled me away. "They fly too fast," she said.

The cotton tops were the animals that finally succeeded in lifting my spirits. I forgot about dead, white-skinned turkeys and cold ovens, and squealed, "Oh, how cute!" when I saw those small, worried-looking monkeys with mops of white fur on their heads. According to the sign, they lived in groups of two females and three males, but only one of the females had the babies. I watched the cotton tops contentedly until Avery complained that he was suffocating in the hot, steamy atmosphere.

We headed for the exit, but a gigantic two-story cage of big black-and-white colobus monkeys stopped us short. Two monkeys were swinging rapidly through their private jungle. Their long white tails plumed out behind them, and the fringe of white hair on their shoulders and back looked like royal cloaks. They were gorgeous animals, but what brought tears to my eyes was the scene on a high tree platform where three adult monkeys crouched, busily grooming each other and their babies.

"Now there," I murmured, "there's a real family."

"Aren't we a real family, too?" Bliss asked.

"I guess so," I said and stopped there, not saying

what I really believed — that if we were, we'd be sitting down to turkey and stuffing at a table with our parents right now.

"I'm getting hungry," Avery said.

"Let's go to the cafeteria. We can see Monkey Island and the polar bears after," Bliss said.

"Or we could grab a sandwich and then go back to Grandma's and finish cooking the turkey for supper," I suggested. The colobus monkeys had revived my energy and determination. But Avery and Bliss eyed me warily. "I'm sure I could do it right this time," I told them.

"Maybe the cafeteria will have turkey," Avery said.

"It wouldn't be any good," I informed him, recalling Grandma's comment about restaurants and dry turkey with thick gravy.

"I like tuna fish better anyway," Bliss said.

"So do I," Avery said. He ducked his head to avoid my eyes.

"You order tuna fish too, Gilda," Bliss said. "Then we'll all be the same." She threw her arms around me. "I love you so much. You're my best sister."

"She's your only sister, dummy. I'm your brother."

"You're the best too, Avery," Bliss assured him.

"Dumb." Avery shook his head. "Really dumb." But he was grinning.

What could I do? I asked myself. They just didn't understand the importance of traditions. Forget it, Gilda, I told myself. Why cook a turkey that nobody but you wants to eat?

I gave up and raced them through a chilly wind to the zoo cafeteria. There I recklessly ordered three hot chocolates and three tuna fish salad plates so expensive that I had to break into the second twenty to pay for them. The cafeteria was empty and we had our choice of seats. Bliss picked a booth surrounded by mirrors and plants with a view of the courtyard.

"Isn't this nice?" she asked.

I nodded, trying to smile as I put down the tray with our food. We each took one of the plastic dishes.

"This is a fun Thanksgiving," Avery announced. He picked up a fork and began to eat, nearly making me choke when he added, "Maybe we could do it again next year."

"You mean go to the zoo?" I asked.

"Yeah," Avery said. "And eat what we want."

"It could be our secret thing, just ours," Bliss said.

"Like our own private celebration," Avery said.

"You mean, make *this* our family tradition?" I asked like the straight man in a not very funny comedy act.

"Why not? I really like the zoo," Avery said.

"Me *too*," Bliss said.

I groaned. Then I stabbed my plastic fork into the pale hump of salad and tasted it. The lettuce was soggy, and the tuna was bland. Tears filled my eyes as I forked down the tuna. It wasn't the feast we should be eating.

16

Grandma was up and about by the time we returned to the apartment. "I'm quite well now, thank you," she said when we asked her how she was feeling. "But I'm afraid the turkey's been out defrosted and uncooked for too long. It's not safe to eat."

She disposed of the bird and took us out to dinner that evening. No one ordered turkey. I didn't object. In fact, I tried the chicken cordon bleu myself. Well, I love things with cheese.

The rest of that weekend went fine. Friday we spent most of the day at the Museum of Natural History. Saturday we tried ice-skating at Rockefeller Center and went shopping. Sunday Grandma took us out for a fancy brunch and then to the train station.

Without any prodding from me, Avery thanked Grandma when she kissed us good-bye. I told her what a wonderful weekend she'd given us, and she said, "I certainly hope you enjoyed yourselves. As for me, this weekend turned into one of the best holidays I can remember. You come down and visit again soon. Promise?"

"Christmas comes next," I said. "And you'll come to us, won't you, Grandma? . . . Well, I mean —" I tried to think which part of the family "us" was likely to be for Christmas. "I mean once we get it organized."

"We'll see," Grandma said. "We'll be in touch. Bliss and I will be calling you both."

"Fine," I said. After one last long, hard hug from Bliss, I picked up my suitcase and followed Avery onto the train. It was crowded, but we managed to find a seat together, even though this time we both had to watch the world going by backward, and we weren't on the river side. All wrong and backward, I thought as I wrestled Avery's backpack and my suitcase into the overhead rack — that was how this whole holiday had turned out. I dreaded telling Dave how right he had been.

Monday morning I found a Christmas scene already up on the bulletin board opposite the main entrance to the school. It showed an old-fashioned country village with a big decorated tree in the center.

I stopped to stare at the display — Christmas! There was nothing I loved better than a beautiful Christmas tree. I bet Pam would have a giant one to match her high ceilings. Mom would no doubt make do with a fake one on a tabletop. Maybe we could have two Christmas celebrations this year, I was thinking when Dave came up beside me.

"You still mad at me?" he asked.

"No," I said. "Did you have a good Thanksgiving?"

"It was okay. How was yours?"

"You were right," I admitted reluctantly. "I couldn't make anything go the way I wanted, not my parents or the turkey or my grandmother or even my brother and sister."

"That's what I was afraid of," he said. "I wasn't trying to put you down, Gilda. I just figured you might be disappointed."

"Well, you were right."

"You already said that. So what happened?"

"What didn't? Grandma got sick, and we had a fire in the stove, and I couldn't get the turkey cooked, and the sweet potatoes turned to mush, and we ended up eating tuna fish salad in the zoo."

Dave laughed.

I socked his arm. "It wasn't funny!"

"You make it sound funny," he said apologetically.

Somehow that made me laugh. Life had been such serious business for me that I had forgotten how good it felt to laugh. In fact, I kept at it so long that kids coming into school began looking at me strangely.

"Anyway," Dave said when I slowed down, "one good thing about Thanksgiving is you get another chance next November."

That sobered me up fast. I looked at the Christmas scene on the bulletin board again and thought about holidays. Probably the way things were going our family wasn't going to have a picture-perfect one for years — maybe never. But was that so awful? I remembered how Bliss threw her arms around me and told me that she loved me, and how happy she and Avery had been at the zoo. Grandma had been happy, too, when she got well, so glad to have us with her. I'd never realized how much she cared about us.

It had certainly been a *different* kind of Thanksgiving — paper bags burning in the oven, uncooked turkey, soggy tuna fish salads, colobus monkeys, and all. But its being different made it memorable in a funny kind of way. So what if we ended up having pizza for Christmas and more than one tree? We cared about each other, and that's what mattered most.

The bell rang for homeroom. "You know what I'm going to do for Christmas?" I asked Dave as we started down the hall.

"What?" he asked me with a worried frown.

"Rejoice!"

Dave grinned. "Hey, Gilda, congratulations. You finally got it right!" he said. And would you believe it? He put his arm around my shoulders and hugged me there in the hall where half the school could see.

About the Author

C. S. Adler lives in Schenectady, New York, where she taught middle school English for many years, and in Wellfleet, Massachusetts. Now a full-time writer, she has more than twenty published books to her credit, including *The Lump in the Middle, Ghost Brother,* and *Always and Forever Friends*. With her realistic and likable characters, her humorous touch, and her keen insight into family relationships, she is a favorite Clarion middle-grade novelist.